THE EN

Enid Richemont was born and brought up in Wales and began writing children's stories to entertain her son and daughter and their friends. In 1989, Walker Books published her first novel, *The Time Tree*. This has since been followed by numerous books for young readers, including *The Dream Dog*, *Gemma and the Beetle People*, *The Glass Bird*, *Kachunka!*, *The Magic Skateboard*, *The Stone That Grew* and *Twice Times Danger*. For older readers she has written *The Game*, *Wolfsong* and *To Summon a Spirit*. Enid Richemont lives in London.

Books by the same author

For younger readers
The Magic Skateboard
The Stone that Grew

For older readers
The Time Tree
To Summon a Spirit
Twice Times Danger
Wolfsong

THE ENCHANTED VILLAGE

ENID RICHEMONT

WALKER BOOKS
AND SUBSIDIARIES
LONDON • BOSTON • SYDNEY

For Jude, Alan, Alfie and Anna – and for some very special people at Constantine School!

First published 1999 by Walker Books Ltd
87 Vauxhall Walk, London SE11 5HJ

This edition published 2000

2 4 6 8 10 9 7 5 3 1

Text © 1999 Enid Richemont
Cover illustration © 1999 Mark Preston

This book has been typeset in Sabon.

Printed in Great Britain by
Cox & Wyman Ltd, Reading, Berkshire

British Library Cataloguing in Publication Data
A catalogue record for this book is
available from the British Library.

ISBN 0-7445-7728-4

CHAPTER ONE

No one noticed the signs, but then, who was looking?

Only Miss Pugh, and who listened to her?

Over at the Goonhilly Telecommunications Centre on the Lizard Peninsula, one of the huge satellite dishes they'd named Merlin registered a tremor so faint it could have been a breath.

But ten miles away, in the village of Tremarion, not even a sea breeze cooled the land during those grey and sultry weeks.

For Piers, all the strange things began when Mum came in from work that day. "Cassandra Pugh's met a flying man," she announced.

"You mean, with flapping wings?" asked Piers. "Like an angel?"

"Not exactly," Mum grinned. "This guy she met in the woods wore his wings on his feet!"

Piers laughed. "Then he'd have to fly upside down."

"Could be," said Mum vaguely, spreading out her newspaper.

Piers always felt a bit confused when they talked about Miss Pugh. Nutty Pugh, some of his friends called her, always seeing spaceships or talking to ghosts. At school they drew cartoons of her driving a flying saucer, or chatting up monsters and little green men.

But Mum liked her. She made a special point of buying things from Cassandra's muddly shop. She'd even put one of Miss Pugh's pink cards on the clinic notice board:

CASSANDRA PUGH
PSYCHIC AND MYSTIC
YOUR FUTURE REVEALED FOR A MODEST FEE

"She ought to write stories," said Piers, who preferred playing football. "So what did he want?"

Mum looked puzzled. "What did *who* want?"

Piers sighed. "Miss Pugh's flying man!"

"Oh, him," said Mum. "Let me see. Yes. He said he had a message for the people of Tremarion."

"Sure, sure," Dad shook his head. "It's those magazines she reads – have you ever seen them?" He topped up his tea. "So what was it this time? Martians taking over the Youth Club? No – they've done that already!"

"The flying man said to tell us the ancient ones are stirring." Mum laughed. "Maybe my physiotherapy's done some of our pensioners more good than I'd realized! Oh, and I nearly forgot," she added, fanning her face with a leaflet that had dropped out of the paper. "He said they may bring us good fortune if we're kind and wise."

"Wise?" Dad shook his head. "That counts me out."

Piers hated the bitterness in Dad's voice.

"*You're* wise, Dad," he said.

"Sure, sure." Dad drank his tea and went outside.

CHAPTER TWO

For the village, the strange things had started much earlier but nobody had noticed, apart from Miss Pugh.

They began with the breaking of soil and the plundering of treasure, then a thin reed of music that wasn't quite heard. Slowly, silently, something netted the land and skies around Tremarion, a thin whisper of magic, a flicker of ancient gold.

Piers looked at Mum.

"The weather's still bugging him," he said.

Mum picked up Dad's plate and mug and rinsed them in the sink. "Well, it hasn't helped."

For so far, it had been a dismal summer. The land around Tremarion seemed wrapped in its own cloud, completely cut off from the rest of Cornwall. You could drive just a few miles away and find blue skies, breezes, summer showers, but in Tremarion that August it had been sullen and dry; warm, but with no sunshine; grey but without rain.

The first fruit on Dad's special apple trees was shrivelled and small, and some of the leaves were already turning brown. They'd turned the hose on twice daily, but it still didn't seem enough. And Dad had to keep spraying against black spot and canker.

"Let's face it," he'd said gloomily. "This isn't working out. Some of those trees are already infected, and now we've got the weather."

"Don't give up yet," Mum had urged, but without much conviction. "Starting a historical orchard was such a brilliant idea." She smiled at Piers now. "See if your dad needs some help," she suggested.

Piers went outside to look for him.

He found Dad hacking at a stave for the windbreak fence. Pippa, their black and white collie, lolled, tongue out, watching.

Piers hung around, feeling useless.

"Want a hand?" he offered.

Dad grunted. "You're not up to this yet, son." He straightened, wiped a fist across his forehead. "It's school holidays," he said crossly, as if Piers didn't know. "Have some fun, why don't you? Find something to *do*!"

Slowly Piers walked back to the mobile home which, for nearly two years, had been where they lived. *The orchard's more important*, Dad had said. *Only when that's a success can we start thinking about building.* It had been fun at first, a bit like camping, but lately everything had begun to feel cramped and small.

"I'll go over to Ben's," Piers told Mum. "Dad doesn't need me." Pippa came leaping and barking, sensing a walk.

"She can come, too," offered Piers. At least that was something.

He opened the gate and walked down the track. He took the short cut through the fields to give Pippa a run, then followed the narrow, winding road that led up to the village of Tremarion. The first sea mist for weeks came curling over the hedges, blurring their outlines, making them float.

"Heel!" Piers shouted, for there was no knowing what might come speeding blindly round the corner. Then grabbing Pippa's collar, he walked her the rest of the way.

Ben was in the front garden, kicking at a football. His cat, Juno, seeing Pippa, bristled, spat, then fled. Unruffled, Pippa took over Juno's warm place.

"Sorry," said Piers. "But she needed a walk. And my dad's in a bad mood," he added, dropping onto the grass.

"The trees?"

Piers nodded.

"Why not grow ordinary apples?"

Piers sighed. "I told you already. The ones we're trying to grow haven't been around for over a hundred years. They're going to taste really special."

Ben shrugged. "Have you heard the latest? Old nutty Pugh's just met a flying man who'll make us all rich." He grinned. "And it's already started. Last weekend, my dad found something in the annexe by the churchyard."

"A body?" suggested Piers.

"Too many," said Ben, rolling his eyes. He went into the kitchen and came back with a couple of cans of Pepsi.

"Sounds creepy," said Piers.

Ben wiped the fizz from his top lip.

"The churchyard's full up," he explained. "So Mr Thompson's been clearing the ground and cutting back the trees in the annexe. And that's where Dad found it."

"Found what?" asked Piers impatiently.

"Bits of a statue. My dad thinks it might be quite old, so he's sent off some photos to the British Museum."

"Wow!" breathed Piers. "So it might be worth a fortune! Show us?"

"Can't. It's in the church," said Ben. "Locked in a cupboard in the vestry. If you came round on Sunday, you could see it."

Piers was embarrassed. "You know we don't."

"I didn't mean that." Ben squirmed. "It's just – I *know* my dad would show you if you told him you were interested. I mean, the cupboard's got a glass front, so it's not meant to be secret. But in the week, he's hardly ever around. He helps out with all these charity things. Mum, too. Hey, wait a minute, though. I know where he keeps the keys."

Piers felt reluctant. "We can't."

"Why not?" Ben grinned. "Dad wouldn't mind, as long as we're careful. Anyway, why should he ever know? My sister's home, but she's up in her room, working on some crazy costume for the fancy dress on Saturday."

They went into the house. The rhythmic chattering of a sewing machine came from somewhere upstairs. Ben pointed out a small room on the right.

"The keys are in there," he said. He pushed open the door and tiptoed inside. "Got them!" he whispered, just as a tall girl draped in swathes of silvery-green glitter came clattering downstairs.

"What do you think you're doing?" she yelled. "You know Dad wouldn't like it."

Ben quickly stuffed the keys in his pocket. "Piers wanted to see."

"See what?" snapped Lucy. "It's only a room. And it's Dad's and it's private. Now will you kids kindly get lost?"

CHAPTER THREE

The boys and Pippa ran up the road and into the churchyard.

"Round the back," directed Ben. "We can get straight into the vestry through the little door."

He unlocked it, and they slipped inside. He locked it again immediately. "Just in case some nosey parker like Mr Thompson spots something. Look, there it is, like I told you. Dad's even done it a label." Ben read, "CARVING. POSSIBLY PRE-MEDIEVAL. FOUND IN ST KEVIN'S CHURCHYARD." It sounded quite grand.

Piers looked. The chunks of stone that made up the small male figure were cracked and mouldy, but he could just make out a head with shoulder-length wavy hair, a curly beard and a broken nose, and pieces of a body with a big chest, no arms, and a few extra pieces that might once have made up all the missing bits.

Ben nudged him and pointed. "He's lost his willie!"

Piers snickered. "Shouldn't be in a church," he joked, "with no clothes on and all."

Ben looked suddenly concerned. "Maybe Dad shouldn't keep it here."

"It's in pieces," said Piers, "so it doesn't count. Can we go into the rest of the place?"

"Come on," said Ben.

Piers followed him into the big echoing space that smelt of damp stone and flowers. A greyish-green light, filtering through plain side windows, fell on the empty pews and the jutting pulpit, the two rows of crumbling pillars, an ancient christening font, and the big collecting box that stood in the shadow of the main door.

"We need money to restore it," said Ben, "but we'll never get enough. The bell tower's got to be fixed, and the roof will cost a fortune."

But Piers was thinking about other things.

"Must be funny sitting here on Sundays," he said, "with all those people listening to your dad."

"Not that many," Ben shrugged. "Anyway, I don't listen. I'm working out tackles and passes and great ways to get goals. I'm thinking about Chelsea or Manchester United." He grinned. "And I'm wondering which one I'm going to sign up for."

There was a sudden flash that made them both jump. Ben ran back to check.

"Lightning?" he muttered as Piers joined him. "It *has* gone dark."

He opened the door, then locked it behind them as they left. Outside, the cloud had deepened into what looked like a winter twilight, yet it was only half past four on an August afternoon. Against the purply darkness, gravestones stood out like bleached bones, and the white bits on Pippa's coat moved like dancing ghosts. Piers thought he heard the faint trill of a recorder or a flute, and wondered if someone with a radio was hanging around the churchyard. There was another flash, then the clouds grew darker.

"It *was* lightning," he said. It felt quite scary. "There's going to be a big storm. I'd better get back."

Over at Goonhilly, no one noticed Merlin half-dipping, then righting itself.

But Merlin's direction had already been fixed, so why should anyone check?

For an instant, the instruments in the control room registered nonsense, and the TV signals on the monitors crackled and spun. But straightaway, everything went right back to normal.

The engineers shrugged. "*Just a blip*," they said.

CHAPTER FOUR

Piers put Pippa on the lead and ran her most of the way. The first heavy drops of rain were falling by the time he'd reached the track.

After he'd opened the gate and run through the orchard, his hair was dripping and his shirt was soaked through.

Dad opened the door and Pippa shook herself all over him.

"Woa, there!" Dad backed off. "I don't need a shower." He was looking more relaxed. "Rain," he gloated. "And about time, too."

Piers towelled Pippa, and then himself. Outside, lightning was flickering, followed by rumbles of thunder.

Mum smiled at Piers. "You got back just in time."

Dad was pointing at the weather map on TV. "That lot are hopeless," he grumbled. "They don't even mention the *possibility* of storms."

"Maybe this is one of those freak jobs." Mum forked a bowl of chopped leeks into the stewpot. "Maybe it's fine over Truro way."

Rain began lashing against the windows. Then lightning jumped and danced, violet and lime, and thunder exploded like a giant bomb.

"That was a close one!" exclaimed Dad.

Piers ran over to look. He enjoyed watching storms, as long as he was safely inside. There was a *crack!* and he ducked, but when he looked again, he thought he saw a big man straddling the sky.

"There's someone up there!" Piers yelled. "Come and see!"

But lightning ripped across his eyeballs, making him blink, and when he looked again, the sky seemed to be empty.

Dad shook his head. "Bad night for flying."

"It wasn't a plane."

"A helicopter, perhaps?" suggested Mum.

But Piers suddenly thought of Miss Pugh and her silly stories. "It was nothing," he told them. "Probably just cloud."

They were settling down to watch a quiz show when the TV went crazy.

"Transmission down." Dad looked smug. "Now they'll *have* to believe in electrical storms." He pulled on his boots, draped his jacket over his head and ran out to check on the trees. The storm waned, then suddenly strengthened, hail stabbing the ground, sending him running back.

"Everything OK," he told them, shaking his jacket outside.

Mum ladled out supper and cut up some bread.

"That's us in for the night," Dad said, locking the door. "I've had enough of that foul weather."

Rain hammered at the roof and rattled at the windows. Lightning flashed again, and thunder growled.

Then, slowly, they became aware of another sound – an urgent rap, rap, tapping at their door.

CHAPTER FIVE

"Something must have worked loose," growled Dad. "No peace for the wicked, not even at supper time!" And he reached for his boots and unlocked the door.

A woman stood outside, a sodden jacket shielding her head, and her long skirts drenched and spattered with mud. Straightaway Pippa jumped up at her and began licking her face.

His cheeks pink, Piers pulled the dog back. "Sorry," he said. "She doesn't usually do that to people she doesn't know." He put his arms around Pippa. "You're supposed to be a watch dog!" he told her.

"Come inside, do," said Mum. "You'll catch your death out there."

"I'm with the fairground people," the woman told them. "We're heading for Tremarion to do a weekend job, but I lost my way in the storm."

"So we'll be having a funfair this year," murmured Mum. "That's nice! Are you by yourself?"

The woman nodded. "But my daughter arrives tomorrow."

"Then sit down," said Mum. "And get some hot food inside you. When this storm's over, you can drive on."

The woman sat. Pippa lay at her feet, gazing up at her adoringly. Piers was puzzled. Pippa was usually shy, reluctant to have anything to do with strangers.

He looked at the woman. She really filled their small chair. She was cushiony and curvy, like his Auntie Susan, and she wore earrings that looked like bunches of grapes. Her face was round and sun-brown and shiny with rain, and her pale hair clung to it in long damp skeins. Piers offered her his towel and she mopped at herself. Then her cheeks grew pink as she began spooning up Mum's stew.

Suddenly she said something that sounded quite odd.

"You make very good use of the fruits of the earth."

"Oh, come on!" Mum shrugged and looked embarrassed. "It's only a stew."

"Where are you parked?" asked Dad.

"In the lane." The woman stood up. "I must be going. You've all been so kind, but I'll trouble you no longer."

"The lady could stay here, couldn't she?" suggested Piers. He never knew afterwards why he'd said it, except that there was something about her he really liked. She seemed to smell of lavender and hay and oranges and peaches. She made him think of hot sun and blackberry pie. He turned to Mum. "She could sleep on the sofa bed we use for Gran."

"Not a bad idea," said Mum. She smiled at the woman. "Fetch your car in the morning. Then you can see where you're going." She put out her hand. "I'm Maggie Baxter, that's my husband, Richard, and the one who had the bright idea is him." She pointed. "Piers."

The woman smiled. "Demetria."

"Is that your name?" asked Piers.

"It's an odd one," said Mum. "But nice," she added hastily.

Dad tried the TV again, but the screen still showed nothing.

"We'll miss the big match," Piers said sadly.

The woman looked at him. "It won't be the same, but I *could* tell you a story." She kicked off her sandals and curled up on the sofa bed, tucking her plump brown toes under her skirts.

Now it was a long time since anyone had told Piers a story.

"OK," he agreed. "Which one will you tell us?"

"I know lots," said Demetria. "But this is one of my favourites…"

CHAPTER SIX

"*Once, long ago, there lived two old people on the side of a hill,*" Demetria said.

"*They were very poor, but that didn't stop them from being happy. They kept a goose which gave them eggs. They grew a few vines and olives and vegetables, and gathered herbs from the hillside, and sometimes a neighbour would bring them a little wine and milk.*

"*One day the King of all the gods came down from Mount Olympus with his son.*"

"Ah," said Mum knowingly. "So it's a Greek story."

Demetria nodded. "That's right."

She went on, "*They disguised themselves as beggars, all tatters and rags. They didn't look very nice and they smelt even worse!*

"*In the rich town at the foot of the hill, they began knocking at doors.*

"'*We are starving,*' *they said.* '*We are cold.*'

"But the grand people in the big houses drove them away.

"'Dirty beggars!' they shouted. 'We'll set our dogs on you!'

"At last, tired and hungry, they followed the trail to the small thatched cottage on the side of the hill.

"When they knocked, the door was opened. Outside, it was dark and cold and it had started to rain.

"'We are starving,' said Zeus, the King of the Gods.

"'And we are cold,' his son, Hermes, said.

"The old women opened the door even wider.

"'We are poor,' she told them. 'But what we have, we'll gladly share.'

"She brought a bowl of spring water for them to wash their hands. Then her husband, Philemon, ladled soup from the pot, and poured out the last drop of wine from the earthenware pitcher.

"'Eat with us,' invited the two gods.

"'We've already eaten,' lied the woman, Baucis, because she knew that there wasn't enough food to go round.

"'But, you must serve yourselves,' the two gods insisted.

"And when Baucis dipped her ladle, she found that the pot was fuller than ever.

"'Drink with us,' invited the gods. And wine

23

came flowing from the earthenware pitcher.

"Then Philemon and Baucis knew that these were no beggars.

"'They must be gods,' whispered Baucis. 'And all we offered them was soup.'

"'I could kill the goose,' suggested Philemon, 'and make a roast.'

"All at once the two gods appeared in their true splendour, and Philemon and Baucis fell to their knees.

"But Zeus smiled and touched their shoulders.

"'No need to sacrifice your goose,' he said. 'We have eaten our fill.'

"'And from now on,' said his son, Hermes, 'you will, too. Follow us,' he ordered.

"They led Philemon and Baucis to the top of the hill, where the night sky glittered with a myriad stars. Then, below them, the old couple saw their cottage with its wooden frame changed into a temple with marble pillars, and its thinly thatched roof shining with threads of pure gold.

"'You took us in and fed us,' the gods told them, 'when others turned us away. Look now at the town.'

"But all they could see was a shining lake.

"'It's under water,' said Zeus. 'But you have been saved because you were kind to strangers. Choose whatever gift you wish and it will be yours.'"

"The old couple looked at each other and then they nodded.

"'We wish for nothing more than to be the guardians of your temple,' said Philemon. 'And that, when our time comes, we might die together.'

"'Your wish is granted,' said Zeus.

"So Philemon and Baucis lived happily for many more years." Demetria smiled. "Then one day, when they were very old indeed, they put their arms around each other and died. And at that moment, Zeus turned Philemon into an oak tree and Baucis into a lime, and their branches twined around each other for ever and ever."

"Ooh, that was lovely!" Mum sighed.

CHAPTER SEVEN

The sun woke Piers early, blazing through the gap between his curtains.

He got dressed, washed his face and went into the main room. Mum and Dad were sitting, drinking tea, and in the middle of the table stood a shining gold apple.

"Demetria's gone," Mum told him. "Just took herself off. But look what she's left you. See?" And she showed him the note, in fine, curly writing, propped against the apple. *For Piers*, it said, *who welcomed me. Thank you.*

Piers picked up the apple, balanced it wonderingly on the palm of his hand. "Is it real gold?" he asked.

Dad laughed. "No one gives that much gold away."

"Then it's a good-luck sign," Piers said. "It means that our apple trees will be OK."

"Not if I don't get some work done," said Dad.

Mum smiled. "You've got a lovely day for it. It's as if that storm washed away all the grey clouds and gloom."

Dad gave Mum a lift to the clinic where she worked. Piers went along for the ride, leaving Pippa behind to guard the orchard.

"Demetria was good at telling stories," said Piers. "But I felt sorry for the people who were drowned in that lake. I mean, they couldn't *all* have been bad. What about that neighbour who brought them wine and milk?"

"The ancient gods were like that." Mum shrugged. "They weren't really kind, but they were very powerful." She laughed. "And they were always having love affairs, or squabbling, like people in sitcoms on TV. We should look out for Demetria on Saturday," she added. "Then you can say thank you for that pretty apple."

"What's going on here?" exclaimed Dad, forced to make a sudden turn because the narrow street through the village was blocked with lines of orange tape.

"Must be an accident. Hope it's no one we know." Mum sighed impatiently. "But this is such a long way round."

At last they drew up in front of the cottage hospital. Mum grabbed her bag and headed for the physiotherapy clinic.

"Sorry I'm late!" she called out to one of the nurses. "We couldn't get through Tremarion.

Main road's blocked."

"I know." The nurse pulled a face. "New Age travellers, they're saying. Or those fairground people. Crazy ones at that. Girl walks up the middle of the road scattering bunches of flowers, roses, lilies, whatever. Cars weave around the place, trying not to hit them. There's a couple of near-misses, but madam doesn't seem to care. Policemen cordon off the road and sweep up the mess, but by then, the girl's long vanished."

"Fairground people," said Mum thoughtfully. "We took one in last night. A woman. I mean, the weather was awful." She pointed at Piers. "It was all his doing!" Then she blew him and Dad two kisses. "Got a patient waiting," she told them. "See you later!"

Dad turned the van round.

"Shell-lime," he said. "I've got to pick up some more from High Cross farm. We can get some shopping done for Mum at the same time, and then maybe go on to Falmouth and eat pasties by the harbour. What do you think?"

Piers nodded. "Sounds great." He enjoyed being with Dad when Dad wasn't grumpy, which wasn't often these days.

They followed the narrow lanes down to the main road, past the turn-off to the cove and the fishermen's cottages. Suddenly, in front of them, a sea-mist seemed to rear up over the road.

Dad slowed, then put on his hazard lights. The tractor behind them did the same.

Fine rain began falling, clouding the windscreen, and behind them, back towards Tremarion, they saw the last of the morning's clear skies.

Dad was mystified. "That's sudden."

At last the mist began thinning, but the sky ahead was still squally.

"Well, we've had our summer," Dad joked. "It happened this morning."

They turned into the farmyard, wheels squelching in mud. Dad got out, disappeared into a barn, then came back followed by another man wheeling a big barrow.

"Shame about the weather," Dad said to him. "It was so nice early on."

The man looked incredulous. "Over Tremarion way? You're joking! It was rotten round here!"

They loaded four heavy sacks into the boot of the car.

"No point in going on now," Dad said, "unless you fancy eating soggy pasties in pouring rain. We'll pick up some stuff from the supermarket, then go straight home."

They shopped, then headed back to Tremarion, but a short way from Falmouth they suddenly moved back into blue skies and sunshine.

"Crazy!" Dad tuned in to a weather report: *Heavy showers and wind over Cornwall and the south-west.*

"But not where we live!" Piers sang.

"Well, it's about time." Dad sighed. "We deserve a bit of summer."

They made sandwiches for lunch and took them outside, spreading out an oilskin because the ground was still damp after last night's storm. Now butterflies frolicked, and bees droned lazily, and from somewhere, Piers again thought he could hear the faint sound of a flute. They sprawled, looking up at the soft blue sky. Dad pointed at the trees with their undersized apples.

"The leaves already look healthier," he remarked, "after all that rain." He sighed heavily. "But it's the fruit we're after."

"Maybe next year?" said Piers.

"Tremarion could have apple fairs," murmured Dad, "if we can get it to work. They used to have them in England, you know – like the wine fêtes in France. Sell honey from our hives as well." He sighed. "'Cornish honey from Baxter's historical orchard' – sounds good!"

"Make cider," suggested Piers.

But Dad scowled. "Not with those precious apples."

CHAPTER EIGHT

They heard the squeak-squeak of the gate. Then Pippa started barking.

"Hi!" called Ben, bumping over the grass on his mountain bike. "Our TV went down last night and we missed the big match. Did you get to see it?"

Piers shook his head. "Ours was out, too."

Ben laid his bike on the grass and squatted down beside them. "Miss Pugh told my sister the fairground people are coming this afternoon," he said.

Dad looked puzzled. "How would she know?"

"Anyway, we already met one," said Piers smugly. "She stayed with us last night."

Ben looked disbelieving. "You haven't got room."

"My Gran stays here sometimes," Piers told him indignantly. "And so does my auntie." He grinned and spread out his hands. "And she's *really* big!"

"Maybe Auntie Susan is." Dad frowned. "But she wouldn't thank you for saying so!"

"I don't mind fat ladies." Piers thought affectionately of Demetria. "They don't bother me."

"Did you hear about the crazy girl?" said Ben. "The one who made flowers grow all the way up the road?"

"*Grow?*" Dad laughed. "They were *bunches* of flowers. We heard about it this morning. Caused traffic chaos and made Piers' mum late for work."

"Well, some of them have rooted," said Ben. "The middle of that road looks just like a garden. It's wild! People are saying it's a stunt to do with the fair. Other people are just mad because they couldn't park their cars."

Dad got up. "Ben, you're beginning to sound like Miss Pugh. They were cut flowers! Anyway, plants can't root in a couple of hours – *you* know that." He grinned. "And I'm much too busy to stay and listen to your nonsense."

Ben punched Piers lightly. "Coming?"

Piers gave him a hard look. "OK," he said. "I'll go and get my bike."

They pedalled down the lane and out to the road.

"Someone came to our house last night, too," Ben told him. "This funny-looking bloke in a crash helmet and weird sandals. Said he and his boss were lost. His gear was drenched. My dad sent him down to the pub."

"But the weather was awful!" exclaimed Piers. He pedalled on silently. Then he said, "You made that stuff up, about the flowers, didn't you?"

But Ben grinned. "Want a bet?"

At the entrance to the main street, the road was still blocked, but now there was a proper sign, with arrows that said DIVERSION. A few cars had pulled up onto the verge, their drivers talking angrily.

"New Age travellers," one of them was saying. "Or those road protesters. Bet they've got a hand in this."

The boys got off their bikes and wheeled them in past the sign. It was strange to see the main street without any cars.

Outside The Fiddler's Arms, a crowd had gathered, spreading down the narrow pavement as far as the post office and spilling out over the road.

"It's vandalism!" someone said, pointing at the cracks in the tarmac.

"Maybe they're trying to say something important," a woman suggested. "There's far too much fast traffic going through this village. One day, someone's going to get hurt."

The boys pushed their bikes up the middle

of the road. The air was warm, and heavy with the scent of flowers. Piers stared at the roses and lavender and white and orange lilies, their stems springing up through jagged splits in the road.

"This can't happen," he cried.

But Ben pulled a face and said, "Wish we'd had a bet!"

Outside her little shop, Miss Pugh was holding court. She'd pinned a couple of roses onto her big straw sun hat, and her glasses, dangling from two gold chains, rested on the plump shelf of her frilly nylon blouse.

"She slept here last night," she was saying reverently. "Said she was sheltering from the storm, but I knew better. I knew it was Cora."

"Cor blimey!" quipped a woman.

"Cora or Persephone," went on Miss Pugh, ignoring her. "Demeter's fair daughter."

"Not *Demeter*," protested Piers. "It's Demetria."

Miss Pugh's shadowed eyes suddenly focussed on him.

"I've met Demetria," boasted Piers. "She stayed with us last night and she said her daughter was coming."

"So you are the chosen one," said Miss Pugh in a hushed voice. "Then you may well be blessed. Or cursed. Remember. The ancient ones..." She closed her eyes. "Not like us. Or perhaps too much like us for our own comfort." She opened her eyes and shrugged. "Take your pick," she said.

"What about your flying man?" teased Ben. "And when do we get rich?"

Miss Pugh glared at him.

"Charity begins at home," she said primly. "Remind your father." She looked fierce. "For he has offended."

Ben wriggled uncomfortably. "My dad didn't do it," he said, trying hard to sound flippant. "It was New Age travellers, wasn't it?"

"Travellers, but not new." Miss Pugh turned back to Piers. "You're a nice boy. I like you, and I'm fond of your mother. Beware of their powers," she breathed. "Accept no gift and make no promises."

And Piers suddenly shivered. "OK."

CHAPTER NINE

"Let's go," muttered Ben. "She's nuts. She scares me."

But suddenly, all along the road the message began rippling, "Traffic coming! Get back, back! Onto the pavement."

"Yobs!" someone yelled. "Can't they read the signs?"

There was a sound of drums, then a purple stretch limousine appeared, moving slowly up the road, hooting its horn and flattening the flowers. On its bonnet was a gold mascot like a fork of lightning, and painted along its sides in sweeping scarlet letters were the words JOVE'S JOYRIDES.

"Of course, it's the fairground people!" somebody said. "Maybe they didn't realize the road was closed."

"I don't think *he'd* care," said a woman, pointing at the driver of the stretch limousine.

The windows were down and the boys could clearly see him. He looked really tough. There was a thin leather strap around his bare brown chest, and the warm sun glittered on his big silver helmet.

"Why the helmet?" asked Ben. "It's not a motorbike, is it? And who's the passenger?"

"The owner, I suppose," said Piers. He put on a posh voice. "Mr By Jove."

"Then Mr By Jove," said Ben, "must make pots and pots of money!"

But Piers was already pointing. "Hey, look what's coming now."

Behind the purple limousine came a big truck, again JOVE'S JOYRIDES in sparkly letters all along its sides. Next came a painted caravan pulled by a black horse, and driven by a woman in a soft leather tunic. She was golden-skinned, with long black hair caught back in beaded coils, and a large tawny owl was perched on her shoulder.

Ben was scornful. "It's stuffed. Oh, wow, it's real!" he exclaimed as the owl's head turned and seemed to stare at him.

There was a sudden burst of music from Mr Apollo's one-man band, with drums, nose flute and guitar all being played at the same time by a slender young man in blue jeans, with a circlet of leaves on his head.

Then a float drifted past, covered in flower petals. It carried a girl curled up on a throne of scallop shells, while tame white doves and sparrows circled round her head. With her long fair hair and girdled gown of silvery silky stuff, she was the most beautiful creature Piers had ever seen.

"Oh," he sighed, feeling his cheeks turning pink.

"She's really something, isn't she?" whispered Ben. "My bossy sister puts me right off girls. I mean, I didn't think they could be like that."

People began clapping.

"It's the old Greek gods," someone said. "See? That's what they're dressed up as."

"Then she's Venus, isn't she?" yelled someone else, "with all them scallop shells."

"*Aphrodite* if she's Greek," murmured a scholarly old man.

Next came a wrestler in a lion skin.

Ben looked concerned. "Hope that's not real fur..."

Some little kids started chanting, "Hercules! Hercules!" and the strong man grinned at them and flexed his muscles.

Last of all came a clomping clown with enormous boots, a rainbow-striped hat, and a stuck-on tail that seemed to grow out of his baggy yellow trousers. From time to time he blew a trill on the reed pipes he carried. Then he'd clack about clumsily, like a clattering old horse.

The boys fell in behind him, wheeling their bikes, joining the crazy procession that was making its way through the centre of the village to the meadow behind the primary school.

Across the road, above their heads, coloured banners had been stretched for the past few weeks:

TREMARION CARNIVAL AND STEAM FAIR
BANK HOLIDAY SATURDAY
RAFFLES, AMUSEMENTS, RIDES and
GRAND FANCY DRESS PARADE
BE THERE!

The limousine turned into the field and the chauffeur got out. In his silver helmet, and with his bare brown chest, he looked more like a bodyguard. He bowed, then opened the passenger door, and out stepped a very tall man in a white linen suit, followed by a plump, haughty-looking lady in a long, shiny dress. The chauffeur lifted out two gold-lacquered chairs and arranged them in the shade beneath the oaks.

Then the wrestler started unloading the big truck. He seemed to be doing it all by himself, setting up stalls and even a carousel with mirrors and painted horses.

The boys watched him, amazed. "He *must* be Hercules," Ben gasped.

Piers dumped his bike on the grass. "I'm going to look for our fairground lady," he said. "Keep an eye on my stuff. I'll be right back."

There was a sudden *flash!* like lightning, and a sudden *crash!* like thunder. Then the man in the white linen suit stood up.

"My lady wife and I," he bellowed, "would like to welcome you all to Jove's Joyrides. We trust that a good time will be had by one and all." Then he sat down and lit up a long cigar.

Piers darted around, looking. At last, in a quiet corner, he found Demetria setting out a trestle table with corn dollies and big bowls of nuts and seeds, with raisins, peaches and apricots and baskets of grapes. Her long indigo skirts billowed from her ample hips and her brown toes peeped through her leather-strapped sandals.

A young woman was helping her. She wore flowers in her hair: marigolds and moon daisies.

Demetria smiled at Piers. "This is my daughter, Penny," she told him proudly. "The one I was telling you about. She won't be with me for much longer." Her grey eyes suddenly looked infinitely sad. "Because she always has to go back to her gloomy old husband."

"Is this a sort of theme fair?" Piers asked. "I mean, people said you were dressed up as some old gods." He looked at Cora. "Did you stay with Miss Pugh?"

The girl nodded.

"But she said your name was Cora," said Piers, confused.

The girl looked at him with clear violet eyes.

"Do you have more than one name?" she asked.

"I've got my dad's name." Piers nodded. "It's Richard."

"Well, we, too, have many names," the girl told him. "Greek ones *and* Roman ones…"

"But what about the flowers?" Piers went on desperately. "Was that you, too?"

Demetria offered him some grapes. "There's still good growing soil," she said fiercely, "under that *awful* road."

Piers suddenly remembered why he'd come looking for her. "Thanks," he said, "for the gold apple. It was really nice of you."

Demetria smiled. "It is for you to use wisely."

Piers felt puzzled. How could you *use* an apple made of gold? You couldn't eat it. It was only for looking at. And it wasn't even real gold, just paint or something.

He didn't quite know what to say.

"Well, thanks anyway," he mumbled.

"Find her?" asked Ben.

Piers nodded. "She left me a present," he explained. "A gold apple. I'll show you. It's really cool. She left it on the table with a note for me. My mum found it this morning, after she'd gone. I wanted to say thank you."

But Ben was staring at him.

"A gift" he joked. "Then you'd better watch out."

Piers began to ask why. Then he suddenly remembered Cassandra Pugh's warning: *Accept no gift and make no promises.*

"Old batty Pugh makes all that stuff up," he retorted bravely.

But on that warm summer afternoon, he felt suddenly chilled.

CHAPTER TEN

They rode their bikes back across the common, then took the short cut by the bowling green to the road that led up to the church.

"Coming round to my place?" invited Ben.

But Piers shook his head. "My mum will be home from work. See you!" he called.

He coasted down the slope, enjoying the pretence of flying. Then, as the road levelled out, he began pedalling hard. He felt uneasy. He felt worried.

A present was a present, he was thinking. Did it stop being a present if you gave it back? But you couldn't give a present back; that was mean, that was horrible. Besides, the apple was pretty, and he didn't want to lose it.

He went bumping up the lane. Behind the gate, Pippa began barking joyfully.

Miss Pugh *was* a nutcase, Piers told himself as he fooled around with Pippa. Nice, but batty. All that stuff about Martians, and ancient ones, and men with wings on their feet. So what was wrong with a present?

Yet things *had* become strange. How could that girl have got flowers like lilies to grow on a road? It was hard enough to make trees thrive in a properly prepared orchard. She'd have to break up the tarmac with a drill or something, and she didn't look strong enough to do that. And it wouldn't work anyway. Plants needed soil that was forked over and nourished, and you didn't get that beneath some rotten old road.

Piers found Mum dozing in a deck-chair, browning her legs. When she heard him, she opened her eyes and stretched herself languidly.

"I'm enjoying it while I can," she told him. "Seems we've got the only good weather in the whole of Cornwall."

"Did you see the road?" Piers was still thinking about it. "Did you see the flowers?"

Mum frowned and shook her head. "We saw some of that nonsense from the bus." She sighed. "It took me for ever to get home. I'll be glad when this carnival thing is over and we can get back to normal." She eased herself up. "Richard!" she called out to Dad. "Tea!"

Piers followed her inside. The gold apple was still where they'd left it.

He picked it up. It was so sparkly, like a

Christmas decoration, like something to hang on the tree. He took it into his room and sat on the bed, remembering Demetria's strange words: *It is for you to use wisely.*

Maybe it *was* real gold, he thought. Maybe one day he could sell it...

He heard the electric kettle humming, then Dad stomping the soil from his boots, and coming in. Piers stood the apple on top of some books on his shelf. Then he went out and helped himself to a chocolate biscuit.

"Hi-ya!" Dad greeted him. "What about this carnival caper? That fairground lot will be in big trouble for ignoring the road signs, *and* they squashed the flowers that daft girl left in the middle of the road. Did you two get to see any of their crazy parade?"

Piers nodded, and told him, told both of them, about the purple stretch limo and the lady with the owl, about the man in the lion skin who was as strong as Hercules, about the beautiful girl and the clown, and about Mr Apollo and his one-man band.

"It's a theme fair," he explained

"Thought it was a steam fair," teased Dad.

"They're all dressed up like gods," Piers said. "That's what Demetria told me."

"Nice woman," mused Mum. "I hope you said thank you."

"But where did they come from?" Dad mused. "Someone told me the council had booked an outfit from Penzance – Kelly's Kapers, or something. It doesn't sound like them."

"Well, Jove's Joyrides is better," said Piers. "That strong man they've got could lift a truck!"

Dad switched on the TV. "What, again?" he grumbled. "What do we pay our licence for? A blank screen two nights running?"

"Let's do something nice," suggested Mum. "It's going to be a lovely evening. Why don't we drive down to the beach and make ourselves a bonfire? We could roast potatoes, maybe, and a few sausages. We might even go paddling under the stars."

So just before sunset they set out, Pippa stretched across the back seat with her head in Piers' lap. They parked just above a little cove, and walked down onto the pebbles. The sky blazed orange and strawberry, the colours melting and dancing in the restless sea. They took off their shoes, picking their way gingerly over the stones, until they reached the coarse sand at the water's edge. Then they splashed about, throwing sticks for Pippa. Above them, the sky deepened to mauve, and the first pale stars glimmered.

They were gathering driftwood for the bonfire when they first saw him – the chauffeur with the helmet, water-skiing naked across the bay, slicing a fountain of silver through the wine-dark sea.

"Gone nudist, have we?" joked Dad. "And the boat that's towing him must have a silencer. I didn't hear a motor."

"We didn't see a boat," said Mum and Piers.

Something glittering suddenly rose out of the water and disappeared below the horizon of the cliffs.

"He flew" shrieked Piers, pointing.

Dad struck a match and blew on the flames. "Don't be daft," he puffed.

"But I *saw* him!"

Mum smiled. "It was probably one of those big gulls. They often look quite strange in this half-light – almost like small angels."

In bed that night Piers thought about the flying man, his helmet burning copper in the sunset, his small white ankle wings spread. With those wings on his feet, it must have been the man Miss Pugh'd met, and he *hadn't* flown upside-down. It was as if some of the daft things she'd made up were coming true, and they were all around him.

He fell asleep and dreamed of the pretty gold apple, then heard men shouting and weapons clashing, sword on shield. He saw blood flowing, people being horribly wounded. Then he saw a city burning with a sunset gold flame. He felt the heat of the fire on his face. Then he opened his eyes and blinked into warm, bright sunshine.

"I had this awful dream," he told Mum next morning. "It was about that apple."

But Mum wasn't really listening.

"Tell me later, love," she said, grabbing her bag. "Or I'll miss my bus."

"I'm giving it back to her," Piers told Dad.

Dad looked quite shocked. "What, that nice lady's present? Just because you had a bad dream?" He chuckled. "Late supper on the beach and too much fizzy drink – sounds like the perfect recipe for nightmares."

CHAPTER ELEVEN

"Take Pippa out," Dad suggested. "Nothing like walking a dog in the sunshine to get rid of black thoughts."

It seemed like a good idea to Piers, too, so he whistled for Pippa and the two of them set off across the fields.

The narrow road through Tremarion still looked like an odd sort of garden. The flowers seemed to have recovered from the fairground procession, and looked as if they'd always been growing there. But now the junction had new signs, with arrows pointing away from the village. TREMARION CARNIVAL, they said. PARK AND WALK.

There was a notice outside Cassandra Pugh's shop: CLOSED FRIDAY AND SATURDAY. Piers wondered why. Miss Pugh could have sold heaps of postcards to all those weekend visitors. She might even have got rid of some of her fusty-looking guide books.

He and Pippa turned down a small street, past the council houses, then followed a track that first climbed a rough slope, then suddenly dipped and meandered through steep woodland.

Pippa went bounding off, crashing through the undergrowth and battling with twigs. Piers left the track and vaguely followed, slithering through ferns and ground ivy, aiming for a place he already knew – a big old tree with a rope swing.

Sunlight, filtering through the leaves, made splashes of emerald on the old tyre at the end of the rope. Dad was right, Piers thought, swinging idly and pretending to be Tarzan. It had only been a dream. After all, he'd seen plenty of films with battles in them – he'd probably been remembering some bits out of those. But the gold apple continued to haunt him, and now there seemed to be nothing pretty about it – just a shiny bauble to put away until next Christmas. It looked a bit silly, he thought, alongside his football shirt and badges and Manchester United scarf.

He could put it away, or even give it back, maybe slip it secretly into Demetria's caravan, or tuck it into the middle of one of her baskets of fruit. She wouldn't find it until the carnival was over, and by then she'd have forgotten all about him.

There was a sudden yelp of pain that made him freeze. Then, from somewhere, Pippa began howling. Piers dropped to the ground, his heart pounding. Surely no one would have set a trap in these woods, where people walked their dogs, and little kids played.

He scrambled down as far as the stream and there he found her, lying on her side, whimpering and licking her paw.

He knelt down beside her. "Poor Pippa, poor girl," he muttered, stroking and soothing her. He grubbed up some moss, dunked it in the clear water, then began mopping at the dark blood and leaf mould that covered the wound. It was then that he saw it – a jagged piece of metal from an old rusty can.

They'd need to get her to a vet quickly, he thought desperately, but there was no way he could carry her. At the same time, he couldn't just leave her in the woods.

He tried calling. "Help! Help!" But there seemed to be no one else around. Then an odd little man appeared from nowhere, running down the slope in oversized boots. He knelt down beside Pippa and gently took her paw. He seemed to know what he was doing, because Pippa stopped whimpering.

Expertly, he pulled out the shard of rusty metal. He showed it to Piers. "Nasty!" he growled.

"Can you help me get her home?" asked

Piers. "We'll have to take her to the vet. She'll probably need an injection – that thing was filthy. But she's heavy. Could you help me carry her?"

Under his rainbow-striped hat, the little man smiled. "No need," he told Piers. "She can walk."

Piers stared at him. "You stupid?" Straight-away he said, "Sorry." After all, the man *was* trying to help. Piers found himself staring at his baggy tweed trousers and his voluminous hat. There was something familiar about him. "Hey!" yelled Piers. "You're the clown with the tail!"

"Right first time." The man grinned. "I'm Mr Pan with the tail. And you're the boy with the apple."

Piers gulped. "How did you know?"

"You can't hang around with that lot," said the man, "without picking things up."

Pippa rolled over, stood, shook herself, then began noisily lapping up water from the stream.

Piers was concerned. "She shouldn't get dirt into that cut."

Mr Pan called. "Come, girl." And Pippa came. "Show us your mended place," Mr Pan said, and Pippa rolled over in the leaves. Piers tickled her tummy, then checked on her wounded paw. The pad beneath her foot was clean and unbroken.

"See?" The man smiled at Piers. "She'll be OK."

"How did you *do* that?" gasped Piers. "It was a really bad cut."

The little man shrugged. "Nature heals."

"Not always," argued Piers, "or we wouldn't need vets."

Pippa went racing up the slope to chase a squirrel.

"She's fine." Piers felt grateful. "Thanks, Mr Pan. You're brilliant. *You* ought to be a vet."

Mr Pan was so brilliant, Piers suddenly thought, that he might help Piers with his problem. He sounded so wise. He'd surely know what to do.

"That apple," Piers said. "Demetria gave it to me."

"I know." The little man shook his head. "That was naughty. It was never hers to give."

"I don't think I really want it," went on Piers. "But it *was* a present and you don't give presents back. And it might even be real gold."

The little man squatted with his back against a tree. "Real gold didn't do my old friend Midas much good."

"Who was Midas?" asked Piers.

"A king who was kind to a god. The god gave him a wish. Well, old Midas was a bit greedy, so he wished that everything he touched would turn to gold."

"He must have ended up a millionaire!" exclaimed Piers, but Mr Pan shook his head.

"You have to be careful when a god gives you a present," Mr Pan said. "Like that wish. At first, Midas had a lot of fun running around touching things and turning them into gold. Very soon, his palace was full of gold tables and chairs. All his cups and glasses and plates turned into pure gold. He touched the robe he was wearing and even that turned into gold, which made it very heavy. Then he asked for his lunch." Mr Pan shrugged. "Well, you can guess what happened. How would you fancy a solid gold pizza?"

"I'd sell it," said Piers, "and buy a hundred real ones. Then I'd get someone to feed me. Midas could have done that."

Mr Pan scratched his head. "Ah, well, he didn't think it through. He didn't understand what was happening. He tried to bully his servant for getting things wrong and of course, his servant turned into gold. Then his little girl came running up to him, and he gave her a hug. He shrugged. "Well *that* was a mistake!"

"You mean...?"

Mr Pan nodded.

"Did it come right in the end?" asked Piers. "Or did he touch *himself* and die?"

"The god felt sorry for him, thought he'd learnt his lesson, told him to go down and bathe in the river, and all the gold washed off in the water. Some of it's still there."

"Wow!" said Piers.

"Turned him right off gold, but he still didn't learn much wisdom. Poor old Midas." Mr Pan sighed. "Ended up with ears like mine!" He suddenly whipped off his cap and Piers saw that his ears were big and furry, like those of a goat.

CHAPTER TWELVE

Piers laughed.

"Those aren't real," he said. "Those are just joke ears. I *know*. You can buy them. And you can get stick-on tails, too. You're all dressed up like gods, aren't you? Even your name. Mr Pan. And I knew a bit about Midas. He's in a book at my school. It's a theme fair, isn't it?"

Mr Pan opened and closed his strange golden eyes. "If you say so."

"And it was a silly wish anyway," went on Piers. "If I'd been King Midas, I'd have done a lot better."

"You need to be careful," repeated the clown, "with wishes and presents."

Piers sighed. "Demetria told me to use the apple wisely," he said, "but I don't know how."

"Perhaps you'll find out." From the folds of his baggy jacket, Mr Pan took out a small set of reed pipes and blew a trill of wild music that sent Pippa rolling with delight in the bracken and damp leaves. Then he paused for a breath. "Bring the apple to the fair on Saturday. They're having a little competition, just among themselves." He chuckled. "Perhaps they'll ask you to decide who that apple really belongs to."

He blew on the pipes again. The music danced around inside Piers' head. It made him want to skip and turn somersaults. It made him want to swing through branches like a crazy monkey.

Mr Pan wiggled his goat ears. "Promise?"

"Promise what?" asked Piers.

"To bring the apple." Mr Pan played another trill of music. "To be the judge."

Piers gave in. After all, it didn't *matter*.

"OK, promise," he said.

Then Mr Pan laughed loudly. "The boy has promised!" he shouted as something glittered and vanished through the tops of the trees. "A promise is a promise," he sang out. "Not to be broken!" Then he ran lightly up the steep bank, and vanished through the leaves.

At home, Piers found Ben waiting. He was looking really worried.

"Someone tried to break into the church," he said. "They damaged the big door and it's hundreds of years old."

"It must have been damaged many times before," Dad pointed out. "Doors don't stay around for that long without being in a battle or two."

"My dad's really upset." Ben glanced meaningfully at Piers. They were both thinking of the night they'd borrowed the church keys to look at the broken statue. Had someone followed them in? Seen things worth stealing and come back later? Piers suddenly remembered that strange music in the churchyard. He didn't want the burglar to be nice Mr Pan.

He looked at Pippa lolling in the sun, her coat warm and glossy.

"She hurt her front paw in the woods," he told Dad. "But the clown from the fair came and helped, and now she's OK."

Dad checked her. "Seems to be fine now," he said. "Couldn't have been anything serious." He turned to Ben. "Have something to eat with us," he offered. "Then we'll drive you back."

They made scrambled eggs and toast and ate them outside. The orchard smelt deliciously of hay and clover.

"This seems to be our private summer," Dad mused. "Or the weather men have got it wrong again. They say it's squally showers over Devon and Cornwall…"

"How are the apples?" asked Ben.

Dad grinned. "Not bad, not bad." He took

out his car keys. "We should be going."

They drove down to the vicarage. The boys sat on the back seat, not speaking much.

A couple of policemen were just leaving as they got out. Ben's mum was in the front garden, seeing them off.

"They reckon it was drunks," she said. "A stupid act of high spirits, in every sense of the word." She smiled at Dad. "Thanks for having Ben. We were in such a state! The last thing on anyone's mind was lunch."

Ben's dad appeared, followed by Ben's sister, Lucy, who looked pleased with herself. "Finished my mermaid costume," she announced. "And guess what? There was enough stuff left over for my baby brother."

Ben eyed her suspiciously. "Enough for what?"

"I'm making you something for the fancy dress."

"I'm not going in for that," growled Ben.

"Oh, Ben," said Ben's dad, "don't be such a spoilsport!"

"At least let her *show* you," wheedled Ben's mum. She turned to Lucy. "Go on, love. Get it."

Lucy ran upstairs and came back waving a fabric tube half covered in green and silver scales. She pulled it over Ben's head.

"See? You're a haddock!" she told him, and everyone laughed. Even Piers laughed, seeing

Ben's furious pink face emerging from the scaly tube. "Bet you'll win," Lucy crowed. Then she looked thoughtfully at Piers. "You could be a chip," she said. "Easy-peasy to make."

Ben was struggling out of his fish tube, threatening to tear it.

"I'm not going in that thing," he protested.

"Oh, Ben!" Ben's mum sighed. "And Lucy *made* it for you."

"I said no!" shouted Ben and he stamped off and began viciously kicking a ball.

Piers followed him.

"Get it!" yelled Ben.

Piers ducked as the ball nearly hit him in the stomach.

"Chip?" taunted Ben.

"Rotten fish," yelled Piers, grabbing him.

"Stop fighting, you two!" ordered Ben's dad. "Take your evil tempers out on that football! Go up to the common and have a proper kick around." He handed Ben some money. "And see how that fair's getting on. You never know – you might win a goldfish."

CHAPTER THIRTEEN

People had started coming into Tremarion for a day in the sunshine.

"Better than a foreign holiday," they joked.

They came on bicycles, or walked, leaving their cars on a small piece of wasteland a couple of miles away.

Along the narrow road through the village they stood, staring, pointing, taking photographs, even picking a few blossoms as souvenirs.

From the meadow behind the school came the sounds of the fair.

"They've got it going," said Piers, but Ben didn't answer.

The boys walked past the bowling green and onto the common. People were picnicking on the grass, or sunbathing. The girl who'd been dressed as Venus had changed into a bikini, and some of the older boys from the village were chatting her up. And little drifts of strange music came floating on the warm summer air.

Ben dropped the ball and kicked it. Piers ran after it and sent it back. For a while, they worked silently at dribbling and passing. Then Ben did a perfect header.

"Great!" yelled Piers, returning the ball.

But Ben was sweating. "It's too hot," he complained. "Let's go for a drink. Let's go over to the fair."

They ran across the common and into the enclosure. Some of the sideshows were being put up, but the two carousels were already working – one for little kids, with animals: lambs and fawns and dolphins, and a big glittery one with mirrors, and horses that swung out on gilded poles.

In the corner of the meadow, the man with the helmet was sprawled on the roof of the stretch limo, and the black horse from the caravan was grazing beneath the oaks.

The strong man was nailing up a big coloured sign: CAN YOU BEAT MR HERCULES? TEN PENCE A TRY. He turned, saw the boys and gave a wide, gap-toothed grin.

"Only ten pence," he challenged, waving a huge hammer.

At last they found a stall that was selling cold drinks. The woman behind it was filling plastic cups from a large silver urn. When she saw Piers, she offered him one.

He sniffed. "What is it?"

The woman smiled at him brilliantly. She had big copper earrings and her hair was done in little waves and loops.

"Best ambrosia, dear," she told him. "Full of vitamins. Very good for you. Try it. If you don't like it, you don't have to buy it."

"Have you got orange?" asked Ben. "I'd prefer orange."

"You would." The woman picked up an enamel pitcher. "Everyone to his taste, I'm sure," she sneered. "That'll be fifty pence, dear," she told Ben. "And cheap at the price."

Piers took a sip of his ambrosia.

"Wow!" he cried. It tasted of everything he liked best – strawberries and bananas and chocolate and chips. "Try some!" he said, turning to Ben.

But Ben wasn't there.

He must have gone to look at the limo, thought Piers. He reached in his pocket to pay, but the woman stopped him.

"For you, it's free, dear. You're the boy with the apple."

Piers stared at her. "How did you know?"

The woman came round and stood beside him. She wore a long purple dress and gold sandals. Piers suddenly recognized her.

"That's right, dear." The woman smiled

again. "I'm Mrs Jove. The boss's wife. And very little escapes me," she added sharply. "That apple's mine, part of a wedding present. Demetria had no business giving it to you."

Piers felt troubled. Hadn't Mr Pan said something like that?

"Sorry," he muttered. "I didn't know."

"No harm done." Mrs Jove glittered. "When you bring it in on Saturday, you'll know whom to give it to, won't you?" She put an arm on his shoulder. "We can be friends, you and I," she purred softly. "And I always reward my friends." She bent closer. "You can call me Auntie Juno."

Piers burst out laughing. "My friend's got a cat called Juno."

"Really!" The woman's face flushed. "You should choose your friends more wisely."

"Oh, come on," said Piers. "Ben wasn't to know. And Juno's a nice cat, all ginger and fluffy."

Mrs Jove looked furious. "Don't talk to me about your friend's cursed cat! Did you know my husband's image has been stolen by your friend's family?"

Piers was shocked. "That's rubbish! Ben's dad's a vicar. He doesn't go round nicking things." He pulled away. "I need to find Ben."

"Let's forget your friend," said Mrs Jove. She pointed at the prancing, dancing horses. "Want a go?" she said. "It's on the house."

"That's a girl's thing," mumbled Piers, but secretly he longed to. "Ben might see me."

"But your friend has gone. Look – they've all gone."

And when Piers looked round, he saw that the meadow was empty.

The horses slowed and stopped. Dreamily, he put his foot in a stirrup and swung himself over. The carousel started turning, slowly, slowly, then faster.

"Pick up the gold reins!" It was Mrs Jove's voice. "His name is Pegasus, dear! And believe me, that horse will take you wherever you want to go!"

CHAPTER FOURTEEN

The carousel turned faster and faster. The horse swung out wildly, moving up and down on its gilded pole. Then suddenly it broke loose and rose into the air, and two white wings pushed themselves out from its shoulders.

Terrified, Piers clung to its sleek, warm neck.

"Help!" he shrieked.

The horse turned its head and eyed him scornfully.

"Relax," it said. "Enjoy yourself."

Piers blinked and looked down. He was feeling giddy, and the fair was rapidly becoming part of a pattern of fields. Then the whole of Tremarion was spread out below him. He could pick out the church and the woods behind the council houses. He even thought he could see their own orchard, with the small dark rectangle that was home.

They rose higher and now he could see the ocean, its turquoise and silver crinkles disappearing into cloud. Then there was nothing but cloud, except for the green and gold keyhole slice around Tremarion.

"Where shall we go?" Pegasus yawned. "You're the boy with the power."

"Home!" yelled Piers, thinking wildly, *but horses don't talk.*

"Boring," Pegasus whinnied. "Now, wasn't there a battle you wanted to watch? Fought with a *ball*?" He gave another scornful whinny. "I go for swords and a bit of blood myself, but there's no accounting for taste."

"Manchester United." Piers sighed, remembering. "On TV. But that was two days ago and I missed it."

"Time's no problem," said Pegasus.

There was a sudden flicker – dark, light, dark, light. Then Piers sat, suspended, over a large football stadium.

"Wow!" he breathed. "Have we got the best seats!"

"Who cares?" Pegasus snorted. "I've got better things to think about."

"There's nothing better than football!" yelled Piers.

"Why aren't you playing, then?"

And suddenly Piers was down on the pitch, running, dodging, down in the mud and up again, kicking the ball.

The fans roared. "Goal!" Then they started chanting. "Bax-ter! Bax-ter!"

"That was fantastic!" yelled Piers. Then he sighed. "But it was too easy. I didn't really do it. It was some kind of magic."

Pegasus shook his head. "You think too much. Seems to me you might be better as a trainer. Or even a manager. Why don't you try being a manager? Then you'd have real power."

"Power!" sighed Piers, staring wide-eyed at the flashy gold watch that appeared on his wrist.

Someone came into Piers Baxter's office. It was Ben.

"I'm dropping you from the team," Piers told him. "Sorry."

Ben's eyes filled with tears, which he quickly brushed away. "I could train harder," he pleaded. "We were friends once, remember?"

But Piers Baxter, club manager, was unmoved. "In my business," he told Ben, "there's no room for friendship."

"Power," breathed Pegasus. "That's what Mrs Jove is offering you. Take it or leave it. Now we must go."

Days and nights flickered past as they descended through cloud into the green, sunny island that was Tremarion.

The carousel slowed, then stopped. Piers looked up at the gilded pole and stroked the horse's bristle mane.

"We really flew," he thought. "The horse could talk. I played striker for Manchester. Then I managed the team." He shook himself. "I must have slept and dreamt it."

He scrambled down. Mrs Jove had gone, but Ben was there, grinning.

"Had a nice horsie ride?" he teased.

"Fantastic," breathed Piers. "Want a go? I'll stand you." He suddenly felt very special. "I didn't have to pay," he boasted.

"No thanks." Ben pulled a face, then pointed. "Chip!" he teased.

"Fish!" replied Piers, grinning.

"My sister's a pain," grumbled Ben.

"She's good at making things," Piers pointed out. "I mean, it was a great costume. And there's a ten-pound prize if you win," he added, remembering.

Ben suddenly looked thoughtful.

"If we went as fish and chips," he said, "we'd need more chips. So we'd have to split the prize if we got it."

They dribbled the ball across the common.

"She looked really upset," said Piers, "your sister."

"OK, OK," said Ben. "I'll do it. I'll have to, to please Mum. But only if you come as something, too."

"I'm not being a chip," said Piers.

"All right. But *something*."

And Piers gave in. "OK," he said.

CHAPTER FIFTEEN

That evening, Mum made a big bowl of salad, and set up the picnic table.

Dad brought out a couple of outdoor candles and stuck them into the ground.

"Let's make the most of our private summer," he said. He sounded so much happier since the night of the storm.

They fooled around with a Frisbee, Pippa playing dog-in-the-middle, while the orange sun melted into the distant rim of cloud. Then Mum lit the candles and they sat down to eat.

"That extra shell-lime might be doing the trick." Dad looked pleased. "That, and the rain." He glanced anxiously up at the clear indigo sky. "Hope we're not in for another drought!"

"You're never satisfied," teased Mum. "It'll rain soon enough." She turned to Piers. "I've been thinking about the theme fair," she said.

"And your gold apple. I wonder if they're going to put on something about the Trojan war?"

"What's that?" asked Piers.

"Haven't you read the story?" exclaimed Mum. "Pity. It's a good one. You see, it's the apple that starts the war!"

Piers looked startled. "How?"

"Three goddesses," Mum told him, "had a quarrel. Like I told you, they were always squabbling about something or other. That time, it was about which one was the prettiest."

"Oh, boring," said Piers.

"It doesn't stay that way." Dad took up the story. "They gave a gold apple to a young man, then got him to decide."

"Still boring." Piers spread some pickle on a slice of ham, and remembered playing striker for Manchester United.

"Oh, you're hard to please," said Dad. "Well, the young man chose the prettiest one. Then she gave him a thank-you present. She told him she'd give him the most beautiful girlfriend in the world."

Piers wrestled the Frisbee from Pippa. "So did she?"

"Oh, yes." Dad grinned. "Trouble was, the girlfriend was the wife of the King of Sparta, and he was rather narked. So narked that he got his armies together and set sail for that young man's city – Troy."

Mum brushed away a moth. "It lasted ten years, that war," she said. "And all over an apple."

"It was a *gold* apple," Piers argued.

"Just like yours." Mum smiled. "Perhaps on Saturday, they'll be selling them as souvenirs."

In his room, Piers picked up the apple and turned it over in his hands.

So that's all it was, he thought. A fairground prize, a souvenir, like one of those fluffy rabbits.

And yet...

Mrs Jove had thought it important, and so had Mr Pan. And they might choose him to give it as a prize, just like the young man in the story. Had they meant it, he wondered. If they had, then he'd do it. He suddenly liked the idea of being important.

He climbed into bed, leafed through a football magazine, then went off to sleep.

He slept. Then he dreamt.

He dreamt he was on a beach with Ben and some people from his class. It wasn't Cornwall; it was somewhere really hot. The sky was a deep cornflower blue, and the sea was clear as crystal, and in the distance, he could see high mountains and the tall, dark green spikes of trees.

People ran in and out of the water, splashing each other and jumping waves. Then Piers began swimming.

He did a butterfly stroke, moving swiftly away from the others. Then he rested, floating, the sun warm on his eyelids.

Suddenly someone said, "Hi!"

He rolled over and looked into a girl's face.

"I was swimming beside you," she told him, "but you never noticed."

He noticed now, because the girl was so pretty. Her long fair hair fanned out as she swam alongside him, and as her face turned towards him, she blushed and smiled.

They came to a small island and clambered out. Piers noticed the silver sash looped over her turquoise swimsuit.

And at that moment, Piers knew that he had a crush on her, and he felt his cheeks flame up because he'd never really thought much about girls before.

"Is that a swimming award?" he asked her, pointing to the sash.

The girl smiled and shook her head. "No."

"Are you at my school?" he said awkwardly. "I've never seen you."

Yet he *had* seen her face somewhere, he suddenly thought.

She picked up a scallop shell from the white sand.

"Does it matter?" she asked him. "We can still be friends."

"But I want you as my best friend," blurted Piers.

The girl gazed at him. Her eyes were forget-me-not blue. "What about Ben?" she asked.

"Oh, Ben's just a boy," said Piers crossly.

"What will you give me," the girl said softly, "if I'm to be your best friend?"

"Anything," said Piers rashly.

"Then give me the gold apple." The girl suddenly looked fierce. "It's mine by right, you know. Give it back to me on Saturday and I'll be your friend for ever." She took a small mirror from a chain around her neck. "Look," she said.

And Piers looked.

He saw himself much older, and hand in hand with a girl. She was almost as lovely as the one who sat beside him.

Then Ben walked past.

"Hi!" called Piers, but Ben ignored him.

"Poor Ben, he's still hurt," explained the girl. "Because I used to be his girlfriend." She sighed. "But now I can't help fancying you..."

Disturbed, Piers looked away.

"It's all yours," whispered the girl with the mirror. "The most beautiful girls will just melt before you, if tomorrow," and her voice grew hard and steely, "you give me back what is mine."

CHAPTER SIXTEEN

Next morning, Piers woke up feeling troubled.

He'd been really mean to Ben. Twice. And even if it *was* only in dreams, he still didn't like it. He and Ben had been friends since First Year Juniors.

And that girl's face was still bothering him. He was sure he'd seen her somewhere, so why couldn't he remember? She was the prettiest girl he'd ever met.

Stupid, he thought, worrying about some girl in a dream. There were better things to dream about. Like playing striker for Manchester.

He got dressed and went outside. The orchard was golden with sunlight, and Mum was sitting at the picnic table with a mug of tea and toast.

"My day off," she said blissfully, "and isn't it lovely? I thought we'd have breakfast outside. Your dad's gone to Truro to try and sort out the telly. Lots of people are going." She grinned. "Even our TV repair man! They've even been calling Goonhilly. If Tremarion's not connected before the weekend, they'll have a riot on their hands!"

Piers spooned up his Frosties. He was still thinking about Ben.

"I've got to have a costume," he told Mum, "for the fancy dress tomorrow."

Mum looked alarmed. "This is sudden," she complained.

Piers squirmed. "I promised. Lucy made Ben a costume, and he's got to wear it."

"What is it?" asked Mum.

"A fish."

"Sounds great," she said. "So what's the problem?"

"None of the other boys are dressing up," Piers explained. "Not from our class. So if I go as something too, then Ben won't look so stupid."

"You don't give me much time," grumbled Mum. "It'll have to be something simple." She frowned. "I know! Since Jove's Joyrides seems to be a classical theme fair, you could go as something Greek or Roman."

"I could be a Roman soldier," suggested Piers.

But Mum shook her head. "Something much simpler."

"Like what?" asked Piers.

"Like a shepherd."

"That's Christmas."

"A *Greek* shepherd, dumb-dumb. We can cut open a sack to make a tunic. Then you'll need a staff – well, Dad's got plenty of canes. And I could try to talk my friend Caroline into lending you one of her goats. You can lead it in on a rope. That'll wow the summer visitors!"

"A goat's not a sheep," Piers pointed out.

"Well, you can be a goatherd, whatever..." Mum muttered vaguely. "We'll have to tie a bunch of herbs to your stick because that's what they do. I've seen a photo of a shepherd in a book about Greece." She nodded. "Herbs, yes. Very ethnic."

"The goat'll eat them," said Piers.

Mum shrugged. "Too bad."

They took the breakfast things in, away from the wasps. Then they walked down to the tool shed at the far end of the orchard. Mum grubbed around, then pulled out an old compost sack.

Piers was horrified. "It's filthy!"

"We'll hang it on the line, then hose it down," Mum told him. "In this heat, it'll dry in no time. And here's your shepherd's staff..." She picked up a cane. "It won't have a wiggly bit at the top." She giggled. "Just as well. We don't want you to be taken for Little Bo Peep."

Piers began wishing he hadn't made that silly promise. Lucy was Ben's problem, not his. If he had a sister, he wouldn't let her boss him around.

Back in the kitchen, Mum went rummaging for a tape, then measured him. Outside, Pippa began barking as the gate rasped open.

Mum and Piers went out to check, and found Ben, his mountain bike propped against the fence, and his eyes pink and swollen.

"Last night, someone threw a stone through the church window." He rubbed his eyes. "And now Juno's gone missing."

"Yobs!" Mum said fiercely. "But your cat will come back. Cats often go wandering."

"Not this one. Juno's a lazybones. She never goes far." Ben sniffed. "I think someone's picking on us and so does Lucy."

"Nonsense," exclaimed Mum. "Whoever would do that?"

"Come and see my costume," Piers said to cheer him up, and Ben followed him to where the hosed-down sack hung steaming in the sun.

Piers pointed. "That's it."

"So what? It's a sack," said Ben glumly.

"I'm going as a shepherd," Piers told him. "A Greek shepherd – Mum's nutty idea. And that'll be my tunic. I'm going with a goat, so I'll look even stupider than you."

But Ben didn't laugh.

"Someone's getting at us," he repeated. "The church door's damaged, there's a hole in one of the windows, and now our cat's gone."

The two boys squatted silently in the sun,

under one of Dad's young trees. Piers, not knowing what to say, began playing with a grass stem, making it squeak.

"Oh, shut up!" yelled Ben.

"Sorry," said Piers. "Juno'll come back," he added awkwardly. "She's probably there now."

Juno? he thought. Wasn't that what Mrs Jove was called? He suddenly remembered how mad she'd been when he'd mentioned Ben's cat. But mad enough to steal it? That was silly. She didn't even know where Ben lived.

Then he heard himself saying it: *My friend's dad's a vicar. He doesn't nick things.*

Mrs Jove only had to ask, and anyone would have told her.

There was the other thing she'd said, too. About Ben's dad stealing her husband's image. She couldn't have meant the broken statue because that was hundreds of years old.

And yet...

"Didn't those bad things start happening," Piers said slowly, "after your dad dug up the bits of statue and put them in the church?"

Ben stared at him. "You daft or something?"

"Someone might have seen them," persisted Piers, "and fancied them."

"Then why didn't they take them?" Ben replied angrily. "The cupboard's not locked. That statue kit's a load of rubbish anyway. I mean, half of it's missing!" He stood up. "I'd better see if Juno's back."

CHAPTER SEVENTEEN

"Poor old Ben," Mum said. "He *is* having a hard time."

Piers imagined losing Pippa, and nodded.

Mum put on water for pasta, and grated some cheese. Then she said, "How about showing me that fair you've all been going on about? I'm feeling quite left out."

So after lunch, they walked over to the village.

Mum exclaimed over the flowers in the middle of the road. "Whoever did this," she said, "was very expert. And I know it's a nuisance, but isn't it nice without cars?"

On the main part of the common, people were preparing the fair – sorting out programmes, checking on trestle tables, chalking out race tracks and fencing off a ring for the Cornish wrestling.

Miss Pugh was already sitting at a table

under an orange-flowered parasol. She'd spread out a small display of crystals and charms, and she'd put up one of her notices:

CASSANDRA PUGH
FORTUNES TOLD
PALMS AND TAROT
£2 ONLY

And a small queue of curious summer visitors was beginning to form.

She looked up and saw Piers.

"You first, young man," she said. She smiled at Mum. "Nice to see you again, Mrs Baxter."

A few people began grumbling. "But that kid's only just come and we've been here ages..."

"And I don't want my fortune told anyway," cried Piers.

"Oh, go on," Mum urged. "It's only a bit of fun."

"It's two pounds," Piers reminded her.

"It all goes to charity," said Miss Pugh virtuously. "But I never charge friends."

Embarrassed, Piers perched dutifully on her old kitchen chair. Miss Pugh reached for his hand. Then she stared at him.

"You are in danger," she told him. "But your friend is in greater danger." She sighed impatiently. "Get his father to remove that thing. It's in the wrong place."

"What thing?" asked Piers.

Miss Pugh half-closed her eyes. "It was made to honour them," she muttered. "Now it must return to them." Her plump, pink face drew closer, and the sunlight glittered on the rim of her spectacles. "As for you," she said, "make a wise choice tomorrow, and you may well prosper. But if you don't..." Her warm breath smelt of peppermint. "Trust no one," she whispered, "but yourself."

"Goodness, what was all that about?" asked Mum as they walked away. "And what choice?"

"Mr Pan told me I might have to give someone my gold apple."

Mum looked pleased. "Then they *are* going to do a thing about the Trojan war! And they want a village boy to do the apple bit, so they're going to choose you. And a very good choice, too," she added proudly, "if I may say so."

"They probably didn't mean it," Piers mumbled. And if he gave his apple to anyone, he thought, he'd give it to that dream girl who wouldn't even *be* there.

"So show me these amazing people," urged Mum.

Piers took her by the hand and led her into the enclosure. People were still gasping at the purple stretch limo, while the fierce-looking chauffeur with the helmet stood, bare-chested, watching them sternly.

"Oh, look!" cried Mum, pointing. "We'll have to come to Mr Apollo's gig – it says it's this evening!" The music man was wiring up speakers, still wearing his circlet of dark green leaves.

"That's Mr Apollo," Piers told her. "He plays a one-man band."

"Well, he'll be playing something a bit more serious tonight," observed Mum. "Goodness, who's that in the tree?"

Piers looked up, then waved. "Oh, that's Mr Pan. He's the one who helped when Pippa hurt her paw."

Mum ran up to Mr Hercules. "This looks almost real," she said, touching his lion skin. She grinned. "I trust it isn't?"

But Mr Hercules looked thunderous.

"Madam," he growled. "Do you think me a coward?"

Mum backed away, still smiling. "Of course not, of course not," she told him sweetly. "He's really playing the part, isn't he?" she whispered to Piers. Then, "Oh, look!" she cried. "There's Demetria! And that must be her daughter."

They walked past the bigger carousel with its jingly music. Piers glanced briefly at the swinging horses, trying to pick out Pegasus. It had been a good daydream, he remembered wistfully, playing striker for Manchester...

"What a lovely stall!" exclaimed Mum, smiling at Demetria. "And how kind of you to leave Piers that pretty gold apple." She picked up a corn dolly. "How much is this?"

"Take it," Demetria offered. "A gift for your hospitality."

Piers suddenly felt a flicker of fear. *More gifts*, he thought, but there was no stopping Mum.

"Oh, it's beautiful!" she exclaimed. "Do you make them yourself?"

Demetria nodded. "I'll show you." She lifted up the one she was working on. "See? You do it like this."

Piers hung around, getting bored. After a while, he wandered off. There were so many more things to see now – monster targets with snakes for hair, Aphrodite's Aquarium, and – best of all – Mr Pluto's Amazing Thrills 'n Spills Ghost Train.

He suddenly became aware that Cora was walking beside him. She pointed at the fearsome painted dog with three heads, on Mr Pluto's stall. "My husband runs that." She shuddered. "It's very scary."

"Not too scary for me," bragged Piers.

Cora smiled. "Then you can try it tomorrow."

"I could try it now," said Piers.

But Cora stopped him. "It's not working yet."

They passed Mrs Jove's drinks stall.

Mrs Jove glanced at Cora. "Ambrosia, dear girl?" She held out two cupfuls. "*And* one for the young man." She gave Piers a glittering smile. "All ready for tomorrow, dear?" Her voice suddenly dropped. "You know what to do."

Piers nodded, confused. He wanted to concentrate on the ambrosia, because it tasted like his favourite ice-cream.

Then, all at once, he remembered Juno.

"My friend's cat's gone missing." He tried to stare accusingly at Mrs Jove.

But all she did was yawn. "Nothing to do with me, dear, I'm sure. But then, I never *did* care much for cats."

CHAPTER EIGHTEEN

Piers turned, and found himself looking into a painted caravan.

The lady with the owl was sitting inside. She peered down at him over her work.

"Sorry," said Piers. "I didn't mean to stare."

"Why shouldn't you?" The lady put down her sewing. "I approve of a lad with healthy curiosity. Come in."

Piers looked round for Cora but she seemed to have gone. And over at Demetria's stall, Mum was still chatting.

And this was a real gipsy caravan, with painted pictures on the outside, of trees and mountains and ladies with no clothes on, and funny-looking things that were half-men and half-horses. It even had a name. PALLAS ATHENE, it said. Piers grinned. If that was meant to be *palace*, then the lady couldn't spell!

He walked up the steps. The owl swivelled its head and eyed him solemnly.

"Can I touch him?" Piers asked. "Or would I scare him?"

The lady smiled. "He knows a friend."

Timidly, Piers put out one finger and stroked the bird's chest. Its feathers felt soft as silk.

Piers sighed. "He's beautiful."

"You like animals," observed the lady.

Piers nodded. "I've got a dog. Her name's Pippa."

The lady put out her hand. "And my name is Minerva," she told him. "But my friends call me Minnie."

"*My* friend's lost his cat," Piers told her.

Minnie raised her eyebrows. "And you think Mrs Jove has stolen it."

Piers gulped and nodded.

"You may well be right," said Minnie. "I'll try to find out. Then I'll tell you tomorrow when you bring me my apple. But now," she stood up, "let me show you my treasures."

Piers followed her. Inside, the caravan was much bigger than it seemed. It had a library of books that stretched back and back, and a telescope and a painted globe on a polished wooden table.

The lacy curtains at the windows showed trees with gnarled trunks and twisty branches studded with black and green glass fruit.

"Olive trees," explained Minnie. She pointed at a large black spider dangling from a thread. "Woven by my little friend, Arachne. Oh, I *do* love animals." She pointed at two snakes curled up on a silken cushion. "They won't hurt you," she murmured as Piers drew back. Then she sighed. "I get homesick for the south." She set the globe spinning. Then she stilled it and pointed. "That's where I come from." She offered Piers the shiny brass tele-scope. "See?"

Piers looked and saw a mountain wreathed in cloud. Then the mountain shrank back into the curve of the earth. He shifted the focus and found himself out in deep space. Cold stars glittered above him, below him.

"The night sky," said Minnie. "That's my home, too..." but her voice was already fading...

Piers was the captain of a great ship moving through space. Constellations whirled around him as he flew faster than light.

He was in perfect control, steering from co-ordinates on the navigation screen.

Suddenly, *Error, Error*, flashed the com-puter.

"Activate my Second in Command," ordered Piers.

Risky, warned the computer. *He is frozen in a time capsule. He must be brought back slowly.*

"But I need him *now*!" shouted Piers. And Ben stood before him, dazed and swaying.

Error corrected, flashed the computer. *We are back on course.*

Then Piers saw Ben falling, as a great roar sounded. "Piers Baxter! Space hero! Discoverer of a new galaxy!"

"It was nothing, really," Piers was saying to the TV interviewer. Then he sighed. "Pity, though, about my friend..."

Piers let the telescope drop, and saw it rolling across the table.

"You gave up too quickly," said Minnie. "What a shame, because you always wanted to ride in a spaceship." She smiled. "So how was it?"

"Fantastic!" gasped Piers. "But what happened to Ben?"

Minnie shrugged. "You can't have everything, you know. But if you choose *cleverness*, then so much is possible. Mrs Jove's gift of power is empty without it, and as for pretty girls..." She laughed. "Clever men get all the pretty girls they want." She drew closer. "Think," she urged him. "All that could be yours, for the price of one small apple!"

CHAPTER NINETEEN

Mum chatted excitedly as they walked back across the common.

"Such an original idea," she said, "having a fair based on stories about those old Greek and Roman gods. They were even selling something called ambrosia." She laughed. "I saw Cora buying you one. I'm sure it's only orange squash with a bit of honey, but didn't it taste good?"

"So you had some, too," said Piers.

"Demetria got some from Mrs Jove," said Mum. "She told me you were being shown round Minerva's caravan."

Piers nodded, trying to puzzle things out. That stuff about space really bothered him. He loved science-fiction films, and flying a space-ship was something he'd often dreamed about. But how could Minnie have known that? And how did she make it happen? Could the tele-scope have been linked up to some sort of video? It couldn't have been magic. Magic wasn't any more true than the old Greek gods.

Then Piers remembered the story Demetria had told, about how everyone who hadn't pleased Zeus and Hermes had got drowned in that lake. *They weren't really kind*, Mum had said, *but they were very powerful...*

And he thought of the apple that had started a war.

"That boy who gave the prettiest goddess the prize," he said slowly, "what would have happened if he'd chosen one of the others?"

Mum shrugged. "It wouldn't have made much difference. There mightn't have been a war, because he wouldn't have met the lady. But the other two would have been furious. Bet they'd have messed things up for him somehow."

Piers shivered. "So he didn't really have a chance."

They turned into the road. "The Ancient Greeks called it fate," Mum said. "You did your best, but if that lot didn't like you..."

Mrs Jove didn't like Ben, Piers thought. But why? It couldn't just be the name of his cat. He remembered one of the stuffy things Miss Pugh had said, about charity starting at home. Well, Ben's dad *had* turned away that weird bloke in a crash helmet.

He suddenly thought of something. Had it been *that* bloke?

"You're very quiet," said Mum.

"I'm just thinking," muttered Piers. *Get his father to remove that thing*, he heard Miss Pugh saying. *It's in the wrong place*. It had to be those bits of statue: there was nothing else.

So Ben's family had done three things. They'd turned away Mr Jove's driver, they'd put the statue in the church *and* given their cat the same name as Mrs Jove. No wonder she was mad!

But then Miss Pugh was always saying weird things. Like you weren't supposed to make promises or accept presents. Well, he'd done both, and nothing had happened to him.

He remembered them all laughing about her flying man.

But then, Piers had *seen* him.

Hadn't he?

At home, the orchard gate was open and the car was parked on the grass.

"Dad's back," observed Mum, fending off Pippa.

Feeling uneasy, Piers went in and dialled Ben's number.

Lucy replied. She sounded quite subdued. "I'll get him," she told Piers. "And no, Juno still hasn't come back."

Piers waited, trying to work out what to say.

"Hi," said Ben flatly.

"Have you put up notices," asked Piers,

"about your cat?"

"All over," said Ben. "But whoever tried to break into the church, I know they've got her."

"Nonsense!" Piers heard Ben's mum say.

"We're going up to the gig later," Ben said bitterly. "Dad thought it would cheer us up because our TV's still down, and anyway, my sister's got a thing about Mr Apollo."

There was a squeal of rage from Lucy. "Oh, shut up!"

"We're going, too," said Piers. "See you!"

"Can we go to the gig?" Piers asked after supper. "Ben's family is going, so I told him we would."

"Mr Apollo's gig? Wouldn't miss it!" said Mum.

"Can't park," Dad reminded her.

"Then we'll walk. It's not that far," Mum said. "And we can take a torch for when it gets dark."

They set out across the field in a coppery sunset, leaving Pippa behind.

A few cars were parked along the verge as they came out onto the road, and already the sound of music hung on the air – not rock, not rap, not country, but something much stranger. They took the track past the bowling green and onto the common. Music vibrated around them, making Piers feel oddly excited. Along with other people from the village, they moved over to the enclosure where shimmering rainbows were arching out of Mr Apollo's stand.

"Special effects," explained Dad. "Must be some kind of laser."

Every girl from Tremarion seemed to be there, swaying and bobbing to the music.

"What's that he's playing?" asked Piers.

"I think it's a lyre," said Mum.

'You mean, it tells fibs?"

Mum laughed, then spelt it. "L-y-r-e. It's an ancient instrument, but someone must still make them."

Piers began looking round for Ben. It wasn't easy. People appeared odd and unfamiliar in the last red glow of sunset, and rainbow colours streaked across faces, making them seem almost savage.

Someone banged him on the shoulder. "Found you!" It was Ben. "We're over there." He nudged Piers and pointed. "See Lucy? I think she's in lu-u-urve!"

Even Dad and Mum started swaying to the music.

"They're all nuts," said Ben. "Let's go for some crisps."

The sky darkened, and the rainbows blazed, and the signs on the other stands flashed crimson and gold.

I've got to tell him something, thought Piers. Warn him. But of what?

"Those pieces of statue," he blurted. "Get them out of your church."

Ben blinked at him.

"You still going on about that?" He grinned. "Listen. No one's going to steal them. My dad's fitted new padlocks to the church doors, *and* a burglar alarm."

"That isn't the point!" yelled Piers. But what *was* the point? The gods were offended? He couldn't say that.

"They've got a ghost train now, look." Ben stopped in front of it's painted awnings. "See that dog-thing with all the heads, and a snake for a tail? *Freaky!*" He turned to Piers. "Want a go?"

Suddenly Piers found himself trembling. "It's not working yet," he muttered.

Then, from one of the painted canvas openings, stepped a man in a dusty black robe. His long, thin hair was white, but as he gazed at the boys, his eyeballs glowed scarlet.

"Who's scared of him?" puffed Ben, as they ran over to the snack bar.

"Not me!" gasped Piers. But when he reached for a packet of crisps, his fingers were shaking.

CHAPTER TWENTY

The gig ended to rapturous applause.

"More! More!" people shouted. But the man with the leaf circlet just smiled, then left.

The light show was over. People began drifting away, and the two families walked back together across the common.

"He was cool!" sighed Lucy.

"He wasn't bad," said Ben.

"Any news of your cat?" asked Dad.

"We're still hoping," said Ben's mum.

"And praying," added his dad. "Juno means a lot to us. We wouldn't want to lose her."

"We saw the man who runs the ghost train," said Ben. "He was really creepy."

"Well, Demetria's daughter's married to him," Mum pointed out. "He can't be that bad."

Piers had forgotten about Cora.

"But she's young!" he exclaimed. "And that bloke was really old."

Mum shrugged. "There's no accounting for taste."

At the road, the two families separated and said goodnight.

"What a sky!" said Dad as they walked across the meadow. "We don't need a torch. We can navigate by starlight." He pointed. "See that shiny planet? It's named for the goddess who won the gold apple."

"Which one was that?" asked Piers.

"Venus," Dad told him.

"But even *she* had to cheat," said Mum as they took the short cut across the field. "She had this magic belt which made everyone fall for her, even if they didn't want to."

"There's a Pluto up there somewhere," Dad said, "but it's too far away to see."

"Which one was he?" asked Piers.

"The god of the underworld," whispered Mum. "He ruled over the dead. That's why your Mr Pluto runs the ghost train."

"That's enough mythology," said Dad. "Or Piers will have nightmares."

But that night, Piers fell into a deep and dreamless sleep.

The nightmares only came with the sunshine.

"Another lovely day," sighed Mum. "Someone up there must like us."

But they didn't like Ben, remembered Piers. And today, the ghost train would be working.

Mum loaded the breakfast things onto a tray.

"Caroline will bring the goat round to the fancy dress parade," she told him, setting everything down on the picnic table. "She'll be in charge of it until you put on your costume. And don't forget to take your apple," she teased.

"Talking of apples," said Dad. "Have you seen ours?"

Piers and Mum noticed them for the first time.

"They're a lot bigger!" said Piers.

"They're certainly looking good," observed Mum.

"They've recovered," said Dad proudly. "I think we're winning."

After breakfast, Mum cut the sack into a tunic and stitched up the sides and shoulders.

"That's it," she announced. "Instant fancy dress! You can wear it over your shorts," she told Piers, tying a soft leather belt around his middle. "With bare feet, you'll be perfect." She tied a bunch of bay leaves onto the end of the staff. "There." She sighed. "I wouldn't know you! Now go and fetch that gold apple, and I'll take a photo."

Piers winced. Things were closing in on him and Ben, he thought, smiling obediently for

Mum. It felt as though the gods had caught them both in some kind of trap.

Were they *real* gods? They acted like real gods – arrogant and mean. After all, Ben's family hadn't *meant* to offend them. His own Dad might well have turned that biker away, or even dug up bits of some old statue when he was planting the saplings. They might have called Pippa Juno. Then would *she* have gone missing?

And he didn't want to go back to the fair – he'd already seen the best sideshows – but he knew he had to: he'd promised. *A promise is a promise*, Mr Pan had sung. *Not to be broken!* He'd be letting down Ben. And Mum would be hurt if he didn't turn up for the fancy dress parade.

Yet Mum hadn't really chosen that costume.

A Greek shepherd?

That was how *they* wanted him.

CHAPTER TWENTY-ONE

Mum packed the tunic and the apple into Piers' small rucksack.

"We'll meet up with you later." She laughed. "Along with the goat."

Reluctantly, Piers walked over to the common. He longed to do *anything* else. Even homework.

But he knew now that he had no choice.

He wandered round the stalls, fingering his pocket money. He bought some football stickers and a couple of books, and a raffle ticket for a trip to Paris.

He walked past Miss Pugh's stall with its tarot cards and crystals. In the middle of reading a palm, she called out, "Good fortune go with you, boy!"

There was still no sign of Ben. And then he remembered. Ben had signed up for the Cornish wrestling.

He walked over to the pitch and found Ben waiting his turn. Piers was just going to call out when Mr Pan appeared from nowhere. The hot sun blazed on his jacket and big woolly hat, making him smell a bit like Pippa.

"How's that dog of yours?" he asked.

"Fine," said Piers.

Mr Pan winked. "You wrestling, boy-with-the-apple?"

Piers shook his head.

"Why not?" Mr Pan blew a trill on his funny reed pipes. "With Mrs J on your side, you'd be a champion!"

Piers hesitated. The offer was tempting. But he hadn't done enough training, and he didn't have the right clothes.

"Can't," he said at last. "This lot have registered."

Mr Pan smiled his crooked smile. "I can fix things."

"But that's cheating," argued Piers.

Mr Pan laughed. "What's cheating? What's cheating?" His laughter faded, and then he was gone.

Piers walked over to the fair, but now, at the opening, stood a woman in blue velvet, with a silver bow and arrows slung across her chest.

She held out a clipboard and a pen. "Sign the petition," she said.

"What petition?" asked Piers.

"The Artemis Society." She glared at him, and her beautiful face became suddenly quite frightening. "We support country sports. Especially hunting."

"No thanks," answered Piers. "Sorry."

He moved quickly away, hurrying past the carousels with their squealing kids.

"Win ten pounds!" shouted the lady at the Aunt Sally stall. "Knock out a monster!" The lady had golden skin and a soft leather tunic, and a tawny owl was perched on her dark, coiled hair. "Ten pence a go…" her voice lowered, "but it's free for friends," and she stood six balls on the counter before him.

Piers looked at the monster heads jiggling on the stand. He was glad they were only painted, because they were really scary.

He chose the scariest one – the one with the big staring eyes and snake-like hair. He took aim, then threw, but the ball went crashing past it.

He tried again. The monster's eyes seemed to glow and it was hard to look away. He aimed the ball wildly, and heard it go *thud!* on the grass.

He dropped the third ball when he thought he saw the hair writhing. His fingers closed weakly round the fourth ball. Then he found he was looking at, not hair, but real snakes, their forked tongues flicking and their little eyes glinting like shiny beads.

The ball rolled off the counter and fell at his feet, but Piers didn't even notice. He reached out

102

for the fifth ball. The monster's painted eyes seemed suddenly enormous, their whites tinged lime, and their pupils spinning, whirling, crimson and green. He felt his fingers freeze, his feet rooting into the ground, his legs stiffening and turning into pillars of stone.

Then something glittering moved between him and the monster, and he saw a hand holding a mirror with a silver frame.

"Turn away," a voice told him. "Aim for its reflection."

He looked in the glass, saw the monster, and the spell was broken.

After all, he thought, the nasty thing was only painted wood.

Piers picked up the sixth ball and aimed at the image in the glass, and the monster head jerked backwards and fell off its stand.

The lady threw down the mirror. Then Piers saw it was Minnie.

She grabbed his arm and swung it high. "A winner!" she cried. "No, a *hero*! Medusa's head wins the big prize!" She pressed a ten pound note into Piers' hand. "You see what a little cleverness can do?" she whispered.

Piers opened his fingers, and there it was. Dazed, he walked over to Demetria's stall, and bought a box of crystallized fruit.

Proudly, he handed over the note.

"That's a lot of money," Demetria said.

"I won it," boasted Piers. "I knocked off

Medusa's head."

Demetria gave him a hard look. "Not without help, I'll be bound." She handed him his change wrapped in a five-pound note. "There's no such thing as free money," she told him.

Suddenly Piers saw her, the girl from his dream, sitting astride a wooden horse in the toddlers' playground.

'Hey!' he called, running over, but she jumped down and left.

Piers went darting through the crowds in search of someone with long blonde hair and an old-fashioned sash round the waist of her sun-dress.

The loudspeakers suddenly crackled, and a voice bellowed: "THE GRAND FANCY DRESS PARADE WILL BEGIN IN FIFTEEN MINUTES. WILL CONTESTANTS PLEASE LINE UP OUTSIDE THE SPORTS PAVILION."

Then Piers saw Mum, looking silly, carrying a stick with a bunch of bay leaves, and Caroline with a speckled goat tethered to a rope.

He gave Mum the box of crystallized fruit.

"Present," he told her.

"Yummy!" she cried, but he knew what she was thinking.

"I won ten quid," Piers explained. "I knocked off Medusa's head."

"Wow!" said Mum. "Then you're a hero."

CHAPTER TWENTY-TWO

Around the pavilion there was chaos.

There were three sets of fairy kings and queens, a wizard, a gorilla, and several infants in animal suits. There were some girls from Piers' class dressed up as a pop group. When they saw Piers, they giggled.

"You coming as something, Piers Baxter?" asked one.

Then a green and silver fish came waddling out of the pavilion.

"Wow!" they cried. "Brilliant! Who's inside?"

But Piers kept his mouth shut, so they didn't find out.

"You'd better change quickly," said Mum. "Then we can give you the staff and the goat."

Piers dumped his rucksack and pulled out the tunic, and the apple went rolling across the ground.

Mum fussed over the belt. Piers felt really silly. "Shoes off," she told him. "Bare feet are more ethnic."

One of the girls picked up the gold apple.

"This yours?"

He hesitated, longing to say, *no*.

"Pretty," said the girl, pushing it into his hand.

Piers stuffed it into his pocket, underneath the tunic.

Then Lucy came out of the pavilion, wearing a fake seaweed bra and a slinky fishtail skirt covered in shiny fabric scales.

"Hi, Piers!" She gawped. "What's that supposed to be?"

"A Greek shepherd," said Piers dismally. "Mum's idea."

"The mermaid can lead," shouted one of the helpers. "Then the big people behind her, and the little ones last."

Piers took the rope tether from Caroline. The goat went along mildly, then settled down to munching the hem of the wizard's cloak.

"Get him off me!" yelled the wizard.

"I can't," Piers cried helplessly. He tugged at the rope, but the goat tugged harder.

Music came blaring out of the loudspeakers, and to scattered applause, the procession moved off.

One by one, the contestants filed past the judges' table. The judges grinned, watching

Piers struggling with the goat.

"So you are...?"

"A Greek shepherd," mumbled Piers, his cheeks flaming.

They pointed at the goat. "But that's a ... oh, never mind," they chuckled. "A Greek shepherd," they announced.

The rough rope began hurting Piers' hand. For a moment, he relaxed his grip. It was long enough. The goat ambled into the crowd, and began nibbling a woman's handbag. The woman screamed, "Get away!" and the goat panicked and fled.

"Come back!" yelled Piers, running.

But the goat seemed to have vanished, and the common appeared to be more crowded than ever. He tried to spot Mum's friend Caroline. She'd be really mad with him for losing her goat. He ran round people, into people.

"Seen a goat?" he gasped, but they just stared at him as if he were nuts.

He stumbled and fell, but no one even noticed.

Someone must have ladled on the scent, he thought, because the air was suddenly filled with an unexpected fragrance. He sat up, and found he'd tripped over a rock.

But there weren't any rocks on Tremarion common.

CHAPTER
TWENTY-THREE

There were rocks all around him now – pale, whitish stone pushing up out of sparse hill grass. And there were little drifts of crocuses, mauve and yellow, and evergreens, and gold-speckled thyme, and soft, grey-blue cushions of richly scented lavender.

Piers stood up shakily. In the distance he could see the bare shoulders of mountains hunched under sweeps of snow. This had to be another of his daydreams, he thought. Or had he knocked himself out?

Two grey doves came flying out of a grove of pines, circled by a noisy flock of chattering sparrows.

Then the girl he'd been looking for came walking behind them. She was more beautiful than ever in her pale, floaty sun-dress with its old-fashioned sash.

She came up to Piers and held out a shell.

"Friends?"

Nodding dumbly, he took it.

"Then remember what I told you," she whispered. "And surely beauty *deserves* the prize?"

"Ah, our young Paris!" Mrs Jove stepped out from behind the trees. She nodded approvingly at Piers. "And suitably dressed for the occasion, I see."

"There's a trip to Paris," said Piers, confused. "Does that mean I've won it?"

When Mrs Jove smiled, all her jewels sparkled like little suns. "Maybe," she said. "And then, maybe not. It depends on your good judgement." Her voice grew fierce. "Take out that apple, boy," she ordered.

Reluctantly Piers took the apple from his pocket. Its golden surface shone under the high mountain sun. Then for the first time he saw the message embossed around it. It said:

For She Who Deserves Me

There was a rustling of leaves, then an owl flew out and settled on Piers' shoulder, making him jump. It flapped its wings, tickling his ear.

"A vote for my mistress," it hooted solemnly, "is a vote for wisdom."

Then Minnie stood before him in her soft

leather tunic and a big brassy helmet with two twining snakes.

She held out her wrist and the owl flew back to her. "You see, he likes you," she said. Then her voice dropped. "You could be a great man," she told him, "with the right friends. And talking of friends, we'll have to do something about finding that cat." She smirked. "*Juno*," she said loudly.

And Mrs Jove looked furious.

But Piers was staring at the girl.

He knew now where he'd seen her.

"That lady who's dressed up as Venus," he said slowly. "Are you her daughter?"

And Venus cheated, he remembered Mum saying. She wore a magic sash to make men fall in love with her. Was that what had happened to *him*?

The girl was smiling. She suddenly looked much more grown up.

"I am Aphrodite," she said. "Or Venus, if you like – that's what the Romans called me." She gazed at him. He'd never seen any girl so pretty, not even in films or on TV. "You know me, Piers," she added softly. "You've always known me…"

Minnie frowned. "Stop chatting him up, and let the boy think. He's got a good mind. He'll know whom to choose."

The girl laughed. "Not you, not Minerva,

not old clever-clogs Athene! Prince Paris gave the apple to Aphrodite. It's mine by right."

"The apple belongs to royal Hera," said Mrs Jove firmly. "And that's me."

Piers' head whirled. "You've all got so many names!" He looked from one to another, and thought fearfully of the apple that had started a war. He wondered how Dad would choose. Or Mum. Or Ben.

He thought of how Gran used to sort squabbles between him and his cousins, when he was much younger. *You must always share*, she used to tell them. *That way everyone can have a turn*.

"When I decide," he said, "will you promise to accept it?"

The three women nodded. "Yes," they said.

"Then a promise is a promise," cried Piers, "not to be broken!" He took a deep breath. "The apple belongs to Mrs Jove."

Mrs Jove looked triumphant "You see? You see?" She smiled glitteringly at Piers. "From now on, dear," she said, "your team will win every battle."

"But that would be boring," said Piers and he turned to Minerva. "Minnie should have it, because of her wisdom."

Minerva held out her hand. "Great thinking, boy! I'll make you a computer genius, or the captain of a spaceship. I'll make you prime minister, or the governor of the Bank of

England – just take your pick."

"But Venus is so beautiful," said Piers, going very pink. "And someone once *did* give her the gold apple."

The blonde girl danced forward, her sundress fluttering. "Then I'll be your friend," she sang, "forever and ever."

"You all deserve it," said Piers quickly. "So you must all share it. You can each keep it for six months, and that's my last word." He grinned because he sounded just like Gran. "And the one to catch it gets it first!" he yelled, and he threw the apple so high that it streaked through the air in a shower of gold.

Someone grabbed him. "*Come on!* You asleep, or something?"

It was Ben.

"You've won a prize," he was saying. "And they found the goat! And I've got your shoes," he added.

Piers pushed his feet into his trainers, fumbling with the laces. "What goat?" he asked. "What prize?"

"Dumb-dumb!" Ben giggled. "Come and see!"

Piers let himself be pulled through the crowds. Outside the pavilion, he could see Mum still clutching her box of crystallized fruit, standing next to Ben's mum.

"Our young Greek shepherd deserves a

consolation prize." A judge in a woolly hat gave Piers a long, narrow package wound about with ivy. "Because not *everyone* has a goat problem." And around them, people chuckled.

"Mr Pan?" gasped Piers. "I didn't see you the first time."

"That's because," said Mr Pan, "I wasn't there." He looked at Piers. "So you made your judgement?"

Piers nodded.

"Well then, it must be finished," Mr Pan said.

CHAPTER TWENTY-FOUR

"I don't know what this is all about," said Mum, "but I do know that Ben's bursting to tell you something." She winked at Ben. "Unless he's done it already."

"I won!" shouted Ben. "First prize. Ten quid for that fish costume." He laughed. "They announced it while you were off chasing the goat."

Ben's mum held out her hand. "Like I said – five pounds in your savings account and two pounds for your sister." She put the note in her bag and handed him three pound coins. "But you can spend the rest."

"Some deal," grumbled Ben.

"You, too," said Mum. "Keep two pounds for your savings. What about your consolation prize?" she added. "Aren't you going to open it?"

"Not now," said Piers. "Later." And he put

it in his rucksack.

"Coming back to the fair?" invited Ben. "I'm bagging a ride on that crazy ghost train."

Icy fear suddenly closed around Piers' heart. "Not a ghost train," he said quickly. "That's boring."

"Bet you're scared," challenged Ben.

"No, I'm not," said Piers. He looked around for Mr Pan, but he'd disappeared.

"Remember that creepy bloke?" Ben said. "I mean, he was really something. And if he can look like that, then the ride must be *wicked*!"

"Why not take Lucy?" suggested Ben's mum. "After all, she did your costume. And the poor girl only came second in *her* section." Ben's mum looked quite cross.

"And Ben came first," said Mum, "and Lucy made his costume. So Lucy deserves a treat."

Lucy turned up, breathless, in jeans and a T-shirt. "Did I hear my name?" she asked.

"We're going on the ghost train," Ben told her. "For laughs! You and me and Piers."

"Not me," said Piers. "Honest. It'll be rubbish," he argued desperately. "Ghost trains always are."

"Go on," urged Mum, picking up his rucksack. "I'll take your things home. So we'll see you in an hour or two." She laughed, "*If* you survive it!"

115

Miss Pugh looked up as they walked past her stall.

"Danger!" she warned, but Ben only laughed. "She's always on about something," he said.

The three of them walked over to the crowded enclosure, pushing past the fierce-looking hunting lady with the silver-moon bow.

They bought candyfloss and fizzy drinks and bags of crisps.

"But where's the ambrosia?" asked Piers.

"They must have sold out," said Ben. "So what? It was only squash and water."

They stood looking at the ghost train. Under the late afternoon sun, the painted monsters looked cheap and garish, and the grinning skulls were just like something for Hallowe'en.

Cora was sitting in the ticket booth, her flower-printed dress and garlands of daisy chains oddly out of place.

"Only two places left," she said, before Ben could ask. She suddenly whipped away their bags of crisps. "Sorry," she said briskly. "You can collect them afterwards. No snacks allowed inside, even if you're offered something." Her voice dropped. "Especially if you're offered something. Or, believe me," and she shook her head, "it will be the worse for you."

A single black car drew up on the rails. Ben and Lucy arranged themselves, giggling, on the crimson padded seat. They waved to Piers. "Coward!" Lucy teased.

There was a burst of coloured smoke and the sound of demonic laughter, and when Piers looked again, the two of them had gone.

Cora smiled. "You made your choice, I hear. And I think it was a good one. It's about time those three stopped squabbling. They've been doing it for over two thousand years!" She handed him a pomegranate. "Souvenir," she said.

"Where are they now?" asked Piers nervously.

"Around," Cora said vaguely. "This is the last ride. We'll be packing up later – we're leaving tonight. Have a last look at the fair," she told him. "Go and see my mum. She approves of you."

Piers wandered over to Demetria's stall, and found her weaving yet another corn dolly. She looked up when he called her, and he saw that she'd been crying.

He felt embarrassed. "What's the matter?"

Demetria dabbed at her cheeks with the hem of her skirt. "It's nothing," she said. "It's just that I'm going to miss Cora. She'll be going with him soon, and I won't see her until spring." She suddenly seemed to notice the pomegranate. "Did *she* give you that?"

Piers nodded.

Demetria reached out for it. "This will look good in my fruit display," she said firmly.

"OK," said Piers, surprised. "I don't much like them anyway." He thought again about Cora and the strange old man. "What's her husband like?" he asked. "He looks a bit scary."

"He's just sad." Demetria shook her head. "You see, he has to cope with all the world's sorrows." She suddenly smiled one of her radiant smiles. "I've got something for you," she said.

"Not another apple," he protested.

"Not that, no." Demetria reached under the stall and hauled up a cat basket. "Here she is," she said. "And none the worse for her adventures." And there, curled up inside, lay Juno.

"Wow!" yelled Piers. "You found her. Where was she?"

"Having quite a time," said Demetria mysteriously.

Piers walked over to the ghost train, carrying the cat basket. But the ticket booth had gone, and so had Penny. A couple of workmen were already dismantling the painted panels, and disconnecting the structure of the metal rails.

"Packing up early," one of them grunted.

"Bad weather coming," said the second.

"But my friends are in there," yelled Piers.

The first man mopped his forehead. "No one in there now, lad," he said. "Stands to reason, doesn't it? And Mr and Mrs Pluto will soon be off home."

Then Piers understood. He'd been tricked by them all. Even Demetria. The gods had won, and Mrs Jove had had her revenge on the family which had insulted her.

He wandered round miserably, still trying to find them, but even Demetria had packed up her stall.

She'd delayed him on purpose, he realized now. To give Mr Pluto time to take them.

He walked out onto the common and sat down on the grass. All around him, people seemed to be leaving.

"Fine weather's breaking," someone said.

"Bloke told me they've got TV signals back at The Fiddler's Arms..."

Ben would have loved that, Piers thought miserably. The World Cup would be on tonight, and he'd have been able to watch it.

CHAPTER TWENTY-FIVE

"Hey!" a girl's voice yelled. "Why didn't you wait for us?"

"Look!" Someone crouched down beside him. "He's got Juno in a cat basket!" And Piers blinked at Ben and Lucy.

"Where'd you find her?" asked Lucy, pushing her fingers through the canes to stroke Juno's ginger nose.

"I didn't," said Piers. "It was one of the fairground people – that woman who stayed with us." He remembered how much Pippa had liked Demetria. "She's really good with animals."

"What about taking back the basket?" asked Lucy.

"I don't think," said Piers, "she wants it."

"Didn't she see our ads?" grumbled Ben.

"Maybe not," Piers said. "But where *were* you?" he demanded.

"Where do you think?" Ben sighed impatiently. "Looking for you!"

They began walking back across the common, Ben hugging the basket. The carnival was winding down now, apart from the fireworks, and everyone seemed to be drifting away.

"What was it like," asked Piers, "the ghost train?"

"Really strange," said Lucy quietly. "I don't know how they did it. We rode down this tunnel with marble pillars, only the pillars turned out to be crying people."

"And those creepy hands kept offering us sweets and things," said Ben. "But we didn't take any. Well, it could have been that weird bloke, and they might have been drugged. And anyway, the ghost-train girl said we weren't supposed to."

"Remember the dog," Lucy shuddered, "with all those heads? And the boat that was moored by that big misty river?"

"There was this boatman," whimpered Ben, "with a big black hood. I mean, you couldn't see his face. I don't think he had one. And then it suddenly got quite boring, didn't it? *You* know." He grinned. "Fake spiders and flappy ghosts and plastic skulls and things. You could even spot the wires that worked them."

"So you didn't miss that much," Lucy said.

At the road, they separated.

"Don't miss the big match tonight," urged Ben. "It's on after the fireworks!" He grinned. "Did you know that the TV's come back? See you later!" he called to Piers. "And thanks for finding Juno!"

The news was on as Piers walked in.

"So it *is* mended!" he exclaimed.

"They all are." Dad looked pleased. "Problem with the signals, not the sets, and finally they've fixed it."

Mum pointed at the long package in its spirals of ivy. "Open your booby prize," she told Piers.

"I'm not a booby," Piers protested.

He unwound the ivy, took off the wrapping paper and uncovered a long, green cardboard box. He pushed up the lid. Inside, with its roots cushioned in a ball of earth, lay a little sapling.

Dad looked at the label. "Hesperides Gold," he read. "Never heard of it, but it must be an apple. *Your* apple tree," he said to Piers. "Tomorrow you can plant it."

Then Mum remembered. "No one asked you," she complained, "to give your gold apple to the prettiest goddess."

Piers shrugged. "I lost it." He couldn't tell her. He wasn't even sure it had really happened. "Maybe they never meant to," he said. He suddenly thought of something. "What was the name of the boy who gave the apple to Venus?"

"Paris," said Mum.

"*Prince Paris*," Piers remembered. "Was he French?" he asked.

"Oh, no," Mum laughed. "Don't you remember? Paris was the son of the King of Troy."

CHAPTER TWENTY-SIX

No one saw them leaving.

Except, perhaps, Miss Pugh, who was up late, listening for owls.

"The ancient ones have gone," she told people the next day. "I saw their messenger flying across the full moon on winged sandals."

The people just shrugged and smiled.

Wasn't that the sort of thing Cassandra Pugh always said?

That night too, the huge dishes at Goonhilly had dipped, then recovered.

In the control room, for an instant, the monitors had gone crazy.

"They did the same thing not long ago," muttered one of the engineers. "This equipment must be due for its annual check-up."

*　　*　　*

Piers, Mum and Dad walked up to watch the firework display.

The fair had already packed up and gone, leaving the meadow behind the primary school oddly small and empty.

"Police must have opened the road for them," said Dad. "Especially that limo!"

"Well, it's closed again now, thank goodness." Mum pointed. "Oh, look," she cried. "There's Ben's family!"

Ben's mum and dad came running. "Thanks for finding our cat" they said to Piers.

"It wasn't really me," said Piers. "It was Demetria."

"All the same," said Ben's mum, "the reward is the biggest bag of chips you can eat."

They all went over to the hot-dog stand.

"Guess what?" said Ben. "You know those pieces of statue you kept fussing about? Well, we got rid of them. Sold them. This afternoon!"

Piers gulped. "How?"

Ben's dad took up the story. "Someone arrived from the British Museum. I'd sent them photographs, but I didn't expect such a swift response. A private collector, too – said the museum had passed on the information. Funny-looking bloke – in heavy boots and a wool cap – in this weather, imagine! A real eccentric, too. Got me to cart the pieces back to the house before he'd agree to look at them." Ben's dad laughed. "Told me he was allergic to churches!"

"He knew his stuff, though," said Ben's mum admiringly. "Said the carving had probably been brought over by ancient tin traders – long before Christianity came to Cornwall. Told us it was only of sentimental value, but that he and his colleague collected such things. Apparently," she added, "it was a statue of Zeus."

"You mean, *Doctor Seuss*?" joked Piers.

"No." Ben's dad laughed. "Zeus was the King of the Greek gods. He had Roman names, too – Jupiter, Jove..."

"Did he run a steam fair?" giggled Mum.

"The man who bought those bits of statue," asked Piers slowly, "what was his name?"

Ben's dad scratched his head. "Blow me if I've forgotten. But his heart was in the right place, in spite of his objection to churches. Paid me in cash – hundreds and hundreds of pound coins and fifty pence pieces! To make up for the damage to the church, he said. Nothing to do with him, I told him. But with that much, we can think seriously about repairing the tower!"

Cloud was moving in from the east, threatening to smudge out the last of the blue sky.

"Oh, look!" Someone pointed. "A triple rainbow!"

"That means showers," said Dad. "Hope they hold back for the fireworks."

The rainbows faded, the sky slowly darkened, and a single star shone low in the clear western sky.

Piers' fingers closed around something in his pocket, and he drew out a small scallop shell.

Venus, he thought.

There was a sudden bang and a *whee-e-e* as the first rockets streaked into the sky. Then someone lit all the Catherine-wheels, setting them spinning. There were *oohs* and *ahs* as more rockets exploded in great glittering chrysanthemums of coloured sparks. There were bangers and ice fountains, then a noisy space battle, and finally, in spluttering, sparkling letters, the words:

TREMARION CARNIVAL

And everyone clapped and cheered.

There was a sudden flash of lightning, followed by a rumble of thunder. Piers looked up, and thought he saw a big man with a cigar straddling the sky.

Then the first drop of rain splashed onto his nose.

"Nice timing!" People laughed.

And then they started to run.